A Stolen Kiss

"I don't believe you've ever been kissed." A grin crossed his lips. "That's it, isn't it? You've never experienced one, therefore you think it's the spawn of the devil."

He moved dangerously near and Lila backed against the edge of his desk, trying to flee. He stood so close now that she felt his warmth and smelled his spicy cologne. Her heart pounded so loudly that she thought it was impossible for her to breathe or think clearly.

"I was brought up to believe a lady was betrothed before she allowed herself to be kissed," she argued stubbornly as he moved even closer. Her voice, scarce louder than a whisper, betrayed her nervousness.

"Such old-fashioned beliefs. There's rarely a chit past sixteen who hasn't stolen an innocent kiss at one time or another," he said, shaking his head, the twinkle in his eye making him even more rakish and handsome. "I think it's time we enriched your education, Miss Appleby."

Jove titles by Patricia Laye

A NOVEL AFFAIR
THE TAMING OF LORD WHITFIELD

The Taming of Lord Whitfield

Patricia Laye

JOVE BOOKS, NEW YORK

THE TAMING OF LORD WHITFIELD

A Jove Book / published by arrangement with
the author

PRINTING HISTORY
Jove edition / April 1992

ISBN: 0-515-10831-6

Jove Books are published by The Berkley Publishing Group,
200 Madison Avenue, New York, New York 10016.
The name "JOVE" and the "J" logo
are trademarks belonging to Jove Publications, Inc.

PRINTED IN THE UNITED STATES OF AMERICA

10 9 8 7 6 5 4 3 2 1

*For the two great loves of my life,
my husband Bill and son Kirby.*

Chapter 1

"MAY A GOOSE have hair! Aunt Maude, come here. You must see this." Not waiting for Maude to move, Lila Appleby began describing the scene taking place outside their house. "Lord Whitfield's coach just pulled up. It's eight in the morning and the nob's still dressed in his evening clothes and looks to be brandy-faced to boot. Not the steadiest on his feet, I might add." Lila clucked disapprovingly as she continued to stare from behind the lace-curtained window in their sitting room, idly occupied in what had become her favorite pastime—spying on her new neighbor, Lord Hugh Whitfield.

"I don't know what you find so unusual in that, love. Your dear father came up the steps to our front door many a morn as the cock crowed." Maude Watson loved her brother's child, but she saw little of his carefree, happy personality in Lila. In fact, her niece grew more reserved every day, and this was not to Maude's liking.

Lila was a lovely young woman, although she tried hard to conceal her attractiveness by wearing sedate gowns like the brown wool she wore today. It made her look like a prim spinster when in fact she was only twenty-one, and while not in her prime, certainly not an old maid yet. Until her father's death, she had been witty, charming, and even a flirt. Maude could name the young swains Lila had turned down, and it made her sad to think of the opportunities missed. Still, Lila remained adamant that she'd never marry without love—a fanciful dream now seeming further and further from reach.

"I can remember many an occasion your father, bless his departed soul, came home in his cups."

"Not with a doxy draped over his arm," Lila said, her voice calm yet persistent. She giggled as she watched the pair stagger up the sidewalk to the door of Whitfield's Brighton Hall.

"You're roasting me," exclaimed Maude, getting to her feet, unable to restrain her curiosity another second. Moving behind her niece, she stared out the window and gasped in shock. "You're right! Have you ever seen such? And in broad daylight! The rascal." She chuckled, amazed more than appalled at the young rapscallion's nerve. "A woman of the evening if ever I laid eyes on one. Just look at that gown—red satin. Plunges almost to her waist with those enormous mounds gaping out like two frog eyes."

Lila nodded. "She is well endowed, isn't she?" It was impossible to take her eyes from the couple. While she didn't consider herself a snoop, Lord Whitfield and his antics had become the only exciting thing in her life lately. With him as a neighbor, there was never a predictable moment. The man was wild as the devil himself, and not opposed to flaunting his wicked ways before all of London either. His house had become a constant whirl of gentlemen and ladies of questionable reputation coming and going at all hours. But this was the first time she'd seen him come home early in the morn with a loose woman on his arm, as bold as you please. "Do you suppose she's his mistress?"

"Don't be silly, child. Lord Whitfield wouldn't pay to keep the likes of that trollop." Maude shook her head emphatically. "No, he's picked her up somewhere on his rounds last evening and now can't get rid of her."

"He doesn't seem to be trying very hard," sniffed Lila, with a twinge of envy, as she watched the handsome lord swoop the black-haired wench into his arms and stagger up the stone steps to his front door. The girl threw her arms around his neck, laying her head on his shoulder, and laughed merrily. "I do believe they are both drunk as sailors. Look at the hussy! Gaggling up at him like a moonstruck calf! How old does she look to you?"

"Who knows? No more than your age, I'd guess." Maude dropped the curtain back in place, moved back to her chair, and sank into its comfort. She picked up her embroidery and began stitching once more.

But Lila did not move from her position by the window. Instead she stared at the couple until they disappeared inside.

She thought of the fun the two must be having, laughing and sharing conversation. She didn't suppose they were in love, but she had once been, and even today the pain was almost too great to bear.

She had loved Edward Nelson and freely given her heart to him, thinking marriage was the end result, never once taking into consideration the fact he was a mere officer in His Majesty's Army and poor as a church mouse. Handsome Edward; to this day she could remember his gay laugh and the cleft in his strong chin.

But Edward was also ambitious, and marrying a girl as poor or poorer than he, regardless of her beauty and wit and undying love for him, simply wasn't in his life's plan. If only the cur had told her that before he swept her off her feet, things might have been different. But no, he waited until Lila was absolutely besotted over him—why he had gone so far as to allow her to begin preparing her trousseau before he ran off with Sir Anthony Jacobs' daughter.

And Hertha Jacobs had been as homely as her name! It might not have hurt so terribly much had she been jilted for a beauty like Lady Sara Culiver, but no, Hertha was plump, plain, and painfully shy. In all fairness the girl was extremely sweet and kind to everyone, or so some said, and was reputed to absolutely worship Edward. Who wouldn't, Lila thought, he was a Grecian god.

The awful truth of the matter was that Edward was mercenary. He was willing to cast aside the great love of his life, and Lila was confident she had been that, to marry money. Hertha Jacobs was rich beyond Edward's wildest expectations, and he was tired of being poor. So he had married Hertha, and Sir Jacobs had wrangled him an appointment to India where he now lived with his wife and two small daughters in marvelous comfort, while Lila withered away in London, her heart broken beyond repair.

Most days she put romance and happiness aside, too busy to be bothered by them, and Edward's halo had begun to tarnish the slightest bit. On good days, Lila could acknowledge Edward was merely a scoundrel and deserved the intense heat of India as punishment for jilting her. That was on the good days. On the others, Lila saw herself as the long suffering martyr who lost love for lack of a pound. But the times which really annoyed her were the ones like today, when the world was lovely, spring was in the air, and she thought of love and wished she had a lover like Lord Whitfield next door.

"He's a handsome rascal, I'll say that for him," Maude said. "Don't you agree?" She studied the girl out of the corner of her eye.

"I really haven't noticed," Lila lied. She had indeed noticed, and her heart quickened every time she saw the black-haired rake approach or leave his townhouse, but she had no intention of admitting that to her aunt.

"Humph! If you ask me, you should be seeking an acquaintance with your new neighbor, rather than gaping at him from behind a curtain. A gentleman of his station could give you a far better living than you'll be earning with this school of yours. In fact, it's about time you invited him over for tea. 'Twould be the neighborly thing to do, considering he does live next door."

Maude had had this conversation with her niece before, always with the same results. The girl simply had stopped showing any interest in men since her father's demise. Or was it when that beau of hers, Edward Nelson, eloped with Sir Jacobs' daughter? The two events happened so close together that she couldn't be sure. And Lila was so closemouthed about everything that Maude couldn't pry a thing from her lips. Maude understood the financial burden on Lila now, but still, the girl needed some gaiety and fun in her life.

Lila, who didn't want to hear any more of the advice, moved away from the window and picked up a tall figurine. "How much do you suppose I can get for this? It's an original Greek piece, isn't it?" She turned it over carefully, studying the statue intently.

"Now, you aren't going to sell your poor mama's prize statue are you?" Seeing the sad look on her niece's face, she softened her voice. "Is money indeed that tight, Lila? If so, I have a few pounds set aside that I could advance you. You know you'll come into the money one day anyhow. I don't know why you won't let me share a little with you now."

"Nonsense, Aunt Maude. We've discussed this before. Things are tight at the moment, but I'll manage." She sighed and stared at the figurine to avoid her aunt's sharp eyes. Being in charge of the household and its financial burdens sometimes almost overwhelmed her, however, she had a very optimistic outlook on life and felt everything would eventually be all right. "Things are about as close as they can get—Cook used the last of the tea this morning, and warm water doesn't taste good after a few meals. The butcher sent a note around yesterday saying that I must pay him at least half of his bill before Nettie can pick up any more meat at his place."

"After all the years your father did business with that man, he could be patient for a while longer," scoffed Maude, shaking her head. "The man is deliberately being nasty."

"No, I don't think so. It seems he had been carrying Father for a good year before he died. If only I'd paid more attention to the financial matters before Father's death, I might have been able to prevent him gambling so recklessly, and today I'd have a little nest egg." Lila moved over to scan the bookcase to see what else she might pawn from the numerous vases and silver trays decorating its shelves. The most valuable pieces of silver had long been taken to the pawnbroker. She finally settled on the Grecian figurine for the present.

"Well, love, you certainly can't dwell on the what ifs in life. You'll make do. Now stop fretting." After pausing a few seconds, Maude tried once more to appeal to Lila. "If you'd only consider a suitor. A husband could end your financial woes forever."

"Aunt Maude, look at my choices: Widower Hoover with seven children or Hawkins McCann with buck teeth and bad breath." She shook her head emphatically. "No. Marriage is out of the question. I don't have a dowry to attract a poor man of good birth, nor the beauty to attract a wealthy one."

Lila moved over to a faded brown chair and sat down, blending into the worn fabric like a sparrow on its nest. "There's nothing to do but pick out a few of the best pieces in the house and take them to Mr. Matlock's. He's been very fair with me in the past and sells the items discreetly. You must admit that his commission is a reasonable one." Her face brightened. "And once I build my school's reputation, all the girls from the best families will be coming here, and I can raise the tuition even higher. I have three girls now, and if I succeed in polishing their manners and musical talents so they make successful marriages, I'll be on my way to financial security. You just wait, Aunt Maude." One of Lila's greatest assets was her inability to stay melancholy for long.

"Don't get your hopes up on making silk purses out of the Penkridge sisters," sniffed Maude. "Those are two pitifully homely girls. It's a shame you had to get them for your first students. I wouldn't lay a copper on either of those girls ever marching down the aisle." She picked up her sewing and began embroidering. "As you know, I haven't entirely approved of your scheme to run this school, but I'm going along with it because you are so determined to be independent."

Lila stood and moved over to the chair where her aunt sat, stabbing at her embroidery as if the needle could emphasize her point. Leaning down she hugged the older woman affectionately and kissed the top of her head, which made Maude jump.

"Oh, Aunt Maude, I love you dearly. You are as excited over this venture as I am, you old fraud. And what choice do we have? I could sell the house and move back to Leeds with you, but I'd pine away for the sounds and excitement of London. Why I'd most likely take to my bed and fade away with consumption before the first winter ended"—she sighed melodramatically—"like dear Mama did."

"Humph! You aren't the least like your dear mother, who had the sweetest nature of any soul ever lived, but was born frail and stayed that way all her life. You're as strong and healthy as a race horse, just like the Appleby you are." She moved away from her niece. "And don't be a kissing on me—you know I can't stand people fawning and hugging on me."

Lila gave her another quick squeeze and jumped back before Maude could slap at her arm. "Honestly, I've never seen such a cantankerous person. Show you a little affection and you get downright mean," Lila teased, for her aunt might be grumpy at times, but there wasn't a more sweet-tempered creature alive.

"You're just bored and taking out your frustration by teasing me. Now shoo, before I show you the real back of my hand. I've got to finish these doilies to cover the spot on the sofa before it wears through. We can't let the Penkridge sisters know we're a bit short of resources, or that tightfisted father of theirs will try and whittle down the fees he's paying."

Lila studied the parlor with the eye of a stranger. While the furniture was good, heavy mahogany and walnut pieces polished until they shone, the brown fabric showed slick spots and bare threads in several places on the upholstered chairs and sofa. But in spite of its worn appearance, the room still held an air of genteel living, with its Aubusson rug and porcelain ornaments. A blaze crackled invitingly in the grate, its sparks reflecting off a brass fire set on the hearth. No, she thought, while the house needed repairs, most flaws were hidden from the viewer's eyes. Mr. Penkridge might think Lila eccentric, but was not likely to realize she bordered on destitute, a fact she wished very much to keep hidden from all three of her students and their parents.

While the Penkridge sisters were homely creatures with very arrogant ways and would pack their music books in an instant should they suspect they weren't in the most aristocratic of homes, she did not worry as much about them as her third student, Jacinda Kingsbury.

Now there was a wild baggage, if ever Lila had seen one. The girl was ravishingly beautiful with flaming red hair, green eyes the color of a cat's, and morals to match, if Lila didn't miss her guess. Jacinda had been removed from her last finishing school under strange conditions, which her mother had skirted over during their enrollment conference, and which Lila had not pursued in her eagerness to fill her class.

Sighing deeply, Lila picked up her embroidery hoop and began working swiftly, awaiting the hour of her students' arrival. The quiet morning between breakfast and their classes represented her only free time in the day. Running a household, even with her aunt's skilled assistance, left her little time to daydream. That in itself was a blessing, she thought, because it was when she was idle that she longed for balls, gentlemen callers, and even perhaps a beau. No, she would not let herself dawdle over such nonsensical notions, as they were surely out of her reach now that she was a penniless young woman.

As Lila embroidered the pink petals of a tulip, expertly making the dainty stitches, her mind wandered again to Lord Whitfield. She wondered what he and the young woman were doing at this moment. And even wickedly tried to imagine what it might be like to be kissed by the handsome rake. Such thoughts annoyed her, and she struggled to keep them in remission, but love, or at least romance, held a certain fascination for her, even though she realized the folly of such dreams.

Swiftly she worked on, letting time race by in blissful peace, free for a while from her worries. The doorbell sounded, jolting her out of her thoughts, and a glance at the clock told Lila her charges were arriving. It was ten o'clock, and they were here promptly on the hour, just as she had instructed. Sometimes she wondered if her charges had the slightest hope of improving, or even if their parents cared. In the case of the Penkridge girls, there was room for a lot of improvement in deportment, but Jacinda was another matter. It was possible her mother merely wanted someone to watch over her for a few hours. She laid aside her needlework and shook her head as though to clear such thoughts from it.

Briskly Lila moved with long graceful strides toward the front entrance. She must work on her attitude if she was to be a successful teacher. However, she secretly acknowledged, it was going to take a lot of praying and a great deal of tongue biting to survive, in spite of how confident she sounded when addressing her aunt.

Squaring her shoulders and standing tall, she placed

her hand on the brass doorknob. Her day was about to begin.

"Good morning, ladies," Lila cried cheerfully as she flung open the door and faced her charges. "Mrs. Penkridge, so good to see—"

A loud shriek sounded from next door and all heads turned to see a young woman dash out of Brighton Hall. As Lila stood horrified, the scene unfolded before their eyes, and she was too stunned to rush the young girls inside before the ruckus exploded.

"Come back here, you little baggage!" yelled Lord Whitfield, dressed only in his trousers and boots as he raced after the girl in the red satin dress.

She hiked up her gown and showed leg to her knees to avoid tripping, uncaring about anything but her escape from his lordship and the butler who followed in close pursuit. Glancing over her shoulder, she saw Lord Whitfield reaching out to grab her and screamed a blood-curdling yell as his arms enfolded her struggling body.

While Lila and her guests stared in disbelief, Lord Whitfield began searching the girl, who hurled words at her captors that made Lila weak in the knees. Jacinda giggled, but there was no reaction from the Penkridges, although Lila sensed Mrs. Penkridge's indignation. She stood, staring mutely, simply too stunned to herd the group into the house and out of earshot.

"Ah ha!" laughed Lord Whitfield, his hand coming out from within the depths of the little tart's gown, holding two silver mugs and what appeared to be

some gold jewelry. A snuff box perhaps, thought Lila
from her vantage point.

"Most likely a servant girl," whispered Lila softly,
trying to lessen the seriousness of Lord Whitfield's au-
dacious conduct. But no sooner had the words slipped
from her lips than his lordship threw the kicking,
screaming girl into his carriage and ordered the driver
to be off. It was then that the laughing girl leaned out
the carriage window and planted a kiss on Lord Whitfield's lips. Her laughter filled the air as the coach
raced off down the street.

Lord Whitfield glanced over to Lila's porch and
called in merry tones, "Top of the mornin' to you, ladies!" His rakish features broke into a broad grin, and
he had not even the decency to appear embarrassed or
to offer one whit of apology. Instead, he merely saluted
the group, turned and stalked back up to his townhouse.

Infuriated at such bold audacity, Lila snapped into
action, snubbing his greeting. Whirling, she rushed her
party into the foyer and out of his sight, closing her
front door none too gently. She heard Mrs. Penkridge's
intake of breath and Jacinda Kingsbury's bold giggle.

The nerve of the man, Lila fumed, feeling heat rise to
her cheeks. But outwardly she remained in control, although her heart raced crazily, and she smiled sweetly,
struggling to lessen the shock of the scene.

"I apologize for my boorish neighbor. I regret your
daughters witnessed such a thing, Mrs. Penkridge. I
can assure you that it isn't an everyday occurrence."

Leading the way into the parlor, she invited the
group to be seated. The girls took their places silently,

curious to see what was about to transpire between Mrs. Penkridge and their teacher. Upon hearing the doorbell, Maude had gathered up her sewing and moved into the back sitting room, so as not to distract the students' schooling.

"Miss Appleby, I think perhaps we should talk in private." Mrs. Penkridge nodded toward the girls and back at Lila. "Innocent young ears don't need to hear what I'm about to say."

"Of course," agreed Lila, afraid she was about to lose her new students before she'd had a fair chance at teaching them. "Right this way. We'll go into Father's study." Turning back at the door, Lila instructed, "Girls, start your lessons. Hortense, you begin your piano lesson, while Idelia, you and Jacinda sing along with her." The noise of their singing and playing would prevent eavesdropping, something she'd suspected them of doing in the past. Taking a deep breath, she led the way across the hallway and into her father's study.

The study, while not a large room, gleamed from recent cleaning, as Nettie prided herself in being an immaculate housekeeper. A large walnut desk sat in front of the wide bay windows, which let light into the room. Lila moved behind it, taking her place in her father's leather chair, careful to sit straight and appear business-like. She gestured to a chair by the desk for Mrs. Penkridge, but the older woman ignored the offer, preferring to stand and glare around the room. The girls' voices broke the silence as they began their music lesson. Lila stepped back to the door and closed it quietly, before turning to face Mrs. Penkridge, who still refused to sit.

"Now, madam, I hope this room affords sufficient privacy for your liking. This was my father's favorite room," she added whimsically, still able to smell his stale tobacco. She hoped Mrs. Penkridge wouldn't notice the vacant spaces on the bookshelves left when she'd had to sell leatherbound classics to raise needed household cash. In an effort to disguise the empty shelves, Aunt Maude had brought in antique vases and framed pictures, arranging them tastefully in the vacant spots. The room really looked more appealing and certainly more feminine for a lady's study than when her father had occupied it and the shelves had been packed floor to ceiling with thick leather volumes.

"Won't you have a seat?" Lila offered for the second time, trying to weaken the woman's hostile frown. It was clear she was agitated.

"It's a little early for tea, but I'll be happy to ring for some, if you'll share a cup with me."

"No, there's no need. What I have to say won't take long, and my husband expects me home soon." Mrs. Penkridge was a large-framed woman, with a huge bosom that swelled out even further as she inhaled before her next words. "I might as well get straight to the point, Miss Appleby. When you advertised in the *Times* offering to tutor young ladies in the finer points of etiquette, I thought you were an answer to my prayers, but things haven't . . ." She groped for her next words, until Lila decided to interrupt.

"I'm dismayed, Mrs. Penkridge, that you might not

be pleased with my work. Miss Hortense and young Idelia have advanced so much in the few short weeks they've been students here." She paused and the musical trio's sounds drifted into the study. "Can there be anything more glorious than the sounds of music from three such angelic voices?" They were a little flat and Hortense played several notes somewhere on the piano other than in the area of their intent, but Lila doubted her confronter knew much about harmony, or even music for that matter.

"Your instruction has been most satisfactory, and the girls are quite taken by you. Even Miss Kingsbury's mother is pleased with her daughter's progress here." She paused before adding, "You know the girl had a bad experience at the last . . . last several . . . ahem . . . schools."

"I am most flattered that the girls are happy, but it perplexes me that you seem unsettled over some matter." Was Mrs. Penkridge about to withdraw her girls? Lila felt her knees grow weak at the thought of such a catastrophe. There was no possible way she could meet the household expenses should this happen. "Have I done something to offend you, madam? If so, I will certainly work to right the matter." It annoyed her to have to humble herself, but there appeared no alternative.

"Indeed not. You have been the model of decorum, Miss Appleby. That is not what displeases me."

Letting out her breath at last, Lila ventured her next question, although she was afraid she knew what was vexing the matron. "Please, pray then, tell me what the difficulty is, so that I might right it."

"Very well, then, it is your neighborhood." The woman stared Lila directly in the eye with a haughty look of satisfaction.

"The neighborhood?" She knew it sounded idiotic to repeat the woman's words. "Park Lane is one of the most fashionable addresses in London. My family has lived in this area for generations and there is none finer." This was indeed true, and while her home was among the oldest in the area and had been built when her father's family was quite wealthy, it was a most commodious address still.

Clearing her throat, the matron continued. "Miss Appleby, it appears I must be perfectly blunt about this matter. While you are correct concerning the location of your home, it appears that your new neighbor is about to ruin the neighborhood."

"Lord Whitfield?" What she had feared was becoming fact. "I apologize for what you and the girls witnessed this morning, Mrs. Penkridge, but it was certainly an unfortunate and isolated happening. Until Lord Whitfield arrived, Brighton Hall was one of the most prestiges addresses in London. I . . . I . . ." she stammered, unable to think of an appropriate response.

She wanted to say that the address was still respectable, that it was that cur of a reprobate who needed to be driven from the city by a mob of irate mothers. In his short residence, she had witnessed any number of young ladies entering his front doors. No doubt most left with far less virtue than at their arrival. But to say that would only upset Mrs. Penkridge more. She also wished she had the courage to point out that Lord

Whitfield always appeared in the company of beautiful young women, and neither Hortense nor Idelia stood much chance of ever attracting his eye. Jacinda, on the other hand, was far more of a risk, but her mother wasn't here complaining. Instead, she clenched her teeth and silently awaited the older woman's next words.

Mrs. Penkridge stood her ground, raising her chin an inch higher, so that her nose was almost horizontal with the ceiling. "No, my dear, Hortense and even young Idelia have come home with other tales of wild carryings-on next door." Looking to Lila for acknowledgment, she saw none. "You must realize that gossip and scandalmongers abound in the *haut ton*, and one must guard their children's reputations cautiously."

"I would be the first to agree with you about that," conceded Lila, trying to think of a way to salvage her dignity, wanting to strangle Lord Whitfield for what he was doing to her school. The thought of the man and his activities made her temper rise. If Mrs. Penkridge knew all that she was privilege to about the young rake's carrying on, she would be even more upset. She had to find a way to appease the matron. "You realize that Lord Whitfield comes from one of England's finest families. He is reputed to be among the wealthiest of the bachelors who reside in this part of England. Your daughters will no doubt encounter him at many of the balls and routs once the Season begins."

"All that may be true, Miss Appleby, and I have no way of protecting them from undesirables at social events, however, bringing them into such close proximity to wild parties and—and the likes of what we witnessed this morning is within my control." Color was rising to her cheeks as she continued. "So here is my ultimatum. Either inform your neighbor Lord Whitfield that he must run a respectable house, or I will withdraw my daughters from your school and enroll them elsewhere in town." Pulling her fur cape closer around her shoulders, she nodded firmly. "Good day to you, Miss Appleby. I hope we understand each other clearly and that this matter will not need to be discussed again."

Gulping to control her temper, yet unsure how she could resolve the issue, Lila showed her guest to the front door. "I will certainly have the matter corrected within a short time." Not having the faintest notion of where to start, she stalled for time. "I trust that you will give me several weeks to get the matter corrected."

"I am a reasonable woman, my dear." She patted Lila's hand, although her smile was less than convincing. "I'll give you a few weeks to shut down his house or to bring his behavior into an approvable mode."

When the door closed, Lila leaned against it for a few moments. Her relief over not having the Penkridge girls withdrawn immediately was so great that she wanted to shout for joy, yet she didn't know how she could possibly resolve her dilemma.

Hurriedly, she moved off down the hallway to find Aunt Maude and tell her what had transpired. The more she thought of Lord Whitfield, the angrier she became. He had plenty of money and could carry on like the uncouth man she knew him to be, but she had responsibilities and obligations to meet. There was no alternative. She'd have to face a confrontation with him. Still stewing over his lordship, she found her aunt in the kitchen, busily peeling a bowlful of apples for Cook.

"Here you are, Aunt Maude. I'm so glad to find you." She dropped down in the chair beside her aunt and propped her elbow on the table, drawing a deep breath. "You'll never believe what's happened."

Seeing the distressed look on her niece's face, Maude stopped peeling, holding the knife in mid-air. "What ails you, child? You look like the king has died."

"It's not that bad, but my news is alarming," Lila answered, reaching into the bowl and removing a peeled apple and taking a bite out of it. Food was always a comfort when one was worried. She munched nervously, scarcely tasting the tart flavor. Her stomach felt knotted and she threw down the half-eaten fruit.

Cook, understanding that Lila wanted to discuss something in private with her aunt, excused herself. "I'll just run down to the greengrocer's and pick up some fresh cabbage for our soup," she said, untying her apron and hanging it on the wooden peg by the door.

"That's a wonderful idea, and while you're there pick up some more potatoes and carrots," instructed Maude. She glanced over at Lila and whispered, "We do have credit there, don't we?"

"I'm not sure. Here, Cook, take this pound note with you, just in case you see something else we need." Lila stood and moved over to the cabinet. Taking down a small blue jar, she removed a banknote and held out what only she knew to be the last money in her household account.

After she confronted Lord Whitfield and finished the girls' lessons for the day, she'd run down to the pawnbroker's with the Greek figurine. The money from its sale should tide them over nicely until Mrs. Penkridge paid her daughters' next month's tuition. The Kingsbury girl's tuition would be the first surplus funds Lila would have for an emergency. No, she would not let Lord Whitfield cause her to lose her source of income!

Lila quickly filled her aunt in on all that had transpired between her and Mrs. Penkridge, finishing by standing and announcing, "That obnoxious man next door will not destroy my school!"

Maude who had listened sympathetically, nodded in agreement. "Fine! Now what do you intend to do about it?" She shook her head sadly and said, "If his dear departed father were here, he'd take a stick to him for such scandalous behavior."

"I'd love to see that," hooted Lila. "If he doesn't settle down and stop his wild antics, I may personally horsewhip him." They both laughed at the thought of the diminutive young woman chasing the robust man around the room with a large leather horsewhip.

" 'Twould be a sight to see," laughed Maude, wiping the tears from her eyes.

Lila strolled over to the wooden peg by the door and took down her cape. No need going upstairs and dressing for the occasion. What she had to tell the rake could be said in everyday attire.

"I'm off," she called with more confidence than she felt, as she marched out the door.

"Lord have mercy on my soul, child. You aren't really serious about confronting the gentleman, are you?" For the first time Maude realized she was serious.

Lila stopped and turned to face her. "Of course I'm going to confront him. There isn't anyone else here to do it." With that she turned and moved through the house and out the front door. She heard the girls continuing with their music lesson. Jacinda must be playing, she thought, absently cringing at the missed notes. "It's a good thing she's beautiful," she mumbled to herself.

Taking a deep breath she opened the front door and closed it quietly behind her. There was no need to let the girls see she was making this venture. If she should fail in her mission, the Penkridge girls were sure to tell their mother. No, the best thing for her to do was to handle this as swiftly as possible. But what was she to say? The man had a right to do as he pleased on his own premises, didn't he? And he a Lord in the house of Parliament, she scoffed to herself. She wondered what his uncle would think of Whitfield's behavior were he still alive. The late Earl of Wickambrook had been a most genteel bachelor and had rarely ever had company.

Lila tried to remember having seen him in the last few years of his life. He had lived past ninety and had spent his remaining years either at his country estate or within the walls of Brighton Hall.

When she had first heard a young nephew had inherited the old earl's estate and title, she had been thrilled. And the first time she saw Lord Whitfield, he had been so dashingly handsome in his tall leather boots that reached to his knees and had cut such a figure in his blue velvet tailcoat and tight trousers that her heart had actually fluttered.

She shook her head now in disbelief that she had been so deceived by Lord Whitfield's stately carriage and demeanor that she had mistakenly thought he would be a gentleman also. No gentleman would behave as he seemed determined to do. True he was a bachelor, but nevertheless, he had no business ruining the neighborhood with his disgraceful capers.

She scarcely noticed how overcast the day had become as she stalked down the sidewalk and up to the entrance of the Whitfield house. She saw the name "Brighton Hall" on the bronze marker set in the brown stone wall by the large oak doors. "I'll brighten his hall," she muttered to herself, jaw clenched as she hammered on the huge brass door plate. The sound of the knocker was scarcely louder than the pounding of her heart while she waited to confront Lord Whitfield.

Chapter 2

ALMOST INSTANTLY the huge door swung open and Lila sucked in her breath unconsciously, the urge to retreat stronger than ever. She still had time to stammer some excuse and leave with dignity. Instead she faced the butler who stood waiting patiently. "I'm Lila Appleby. I live next door"—she nodded toward her own brownstone—"and must speak to Lord Whitfield immediately."

"Lord Whitfield is not up and about yet, Miss. If you would like to call in the afternoon, I'll be glad to relay this information to His Lordship." He stood firm, blocking her entrance.

"Wake him! This matter won't wait." Even she was shocked at her audacity. But if she didn't discuss this matter with him now, her nerve would abandon her, so she stood firm and stared down the butler's frown.

There was a brief moment while the butler hesitated, then accepting his place, he relented and stepped aside, motioning for her to enter the foyer. "Please come in, Miss Appleby. I will show you into the morning room. You may warm by the fire, if you like. His Lordship may be a few minutes." He cleared his throat, as if accenting the inconvenience of her visit.

"I'll be fine, but do remind Lord Whitfield that my time is also valuable and I haven't long to spare." She wasn't about to let a mere butler intimidate her. Quietly she followed him down the long hallway and into a sitting room where a fire blazed invitingly in a huge fireplace.

Without glancing around the room, where the show of wealth and beauty almost stunned her, she walked regally over to a wingback chair near the fireplace and sat down, careful to keep her back straight and her chin up.

Once she was seated, the butler bowed and left the room, closing the huge oak doors behind him. When out of earshot, he sighed deeply before climbing the stairs slowly, with dread in his heart. Lord Whitfield was not going to take kindly to being aroused so early. From his appearance earlier this morning, he had made quite a night of it last evening. But the lady seemed so agitated and upset, plus so determined, he felt compelled to summon his master.

When he reached his master's room, he paused outside hoping to hear some faint stirring from within, but as he suspected, only a gentle snoring could be heard. He tapped softly on the door, but it didn't cause a break in the snoring. Tapping a little harder, he entered the bed chamber and called his master's name, only to be rewarded with an oath.

"Have you taken leave of your senses, Albert? You know better than to wake me." Lord Whitfield sat up in bed and groaned, placing his head in his hands and closing his eyes tightly. "What is the problem? And I warn you, my good man, that if the house isn't burning or your mother hasn't expired, then you'll probably be fired for this disruption of my sleep." He rubbed his temples and stared up at Albert through bloodshot eyes. "What time is it, anyhow? I plainly instructed you not to disturb me before four in the afternoon."

"Yes, sir, I know." Albert bowed again, not too distressed by his employer's curt words. Lord Whitfield was not of the nature to really fire a fellow unless he caught the man stealing.

"Then why in thunderation are you here?" His voice boomed, and he faced the short little butler with a scowl.

"There's a lady downstairs who says that she must speak with you at once on an urgent matter."

"Not concerning that little piece we tossed out this morning, I hope."

"No, sir. This is Miss Lila Appleby." Seeing that the name meant nothing to Whitfield, he continued. "Your next door neighbor."

Whitfield waved the man away. "Tell her to come back later, Albert. She probably wants to solicit a contribution for her favorite charity." He lay back down and pulled the covers over his shoulders once more. "And punch up the fire, my good man. 'Tis a bit frosty in here today."

"I don't think she'll leave, sir. She appears extremely agitated and upset about some matter. If I tell her to leave, I really believe, sir, that she'll storm up these steps and into your bedchamber."

Whitfield opened his left eyelid and peered at Albert questioningly. "What the devil is troubling the woman? I don't recall having ever met her." He looked over at his man. "I haven't, have I, Albert?"

The butler grinned back and shook his head. "I think not, my lord. You haven't been calling on your new neighbors, and Miss Appleby doesn't look the type you'd meet on your rounds at night."

Whitfield swung out of bed. "Well, old chap, it seems I might as well get up and go down to meet this woman. You've aroused my curiosity, and I can see you aren't about to leave me alone until I do your bidding." He started pulling on his pants. "Better bring my razor and a fresh cravat. Don't want to offend the woman."

"Yes, sir." Albert quickly began preparing his master's toilet, fetching his shaving mug from in the washstand.

"What type person is this Miss . . . Appleby, didn't you say? Is she interesting?"

"Not your usual type, sir," replied Albert, continuing to lay out fresh clothes.

"Now what's that suppose to mean, Albert? Do I detect a hint of criticism in that remark?" Whitfield felt horrible and was ready to pick a quarrel with his manservant since he had no one else around with whom to bicker.

"No, sir. I merely meant that Miss Appleby appears to be a lady."

"And my other friends have not been? Is that it, eh?"

He chuckled, knowing he was putting Albert on the spot. Moving slowly to the mirror he looked at his reflection and groaned. "This woman's business had better be important to drag me out of my warm bed the way I feel." Lathering up his stubble, he asked, "Why didn't you send her away, anyhow? Nobody gets by you that you don't want. What's up with this Miss Appleby?"

Albert cleared his throat. "Well, sir, she appeared so distressed and nervous that I sensed her problem was of enormous importance to her. And to be honest, my lord, I don't think she'd have left without being forcibly removed."

"You do paint a picture of an extraordinary woman, my man."

LILA GREW IMPATIENT and was too nervous to sit another minute, so she stood and strolled idly around the sitting room, studying portraits of children playing with dogs, and a picture of a serious young man all dressed up in his starched finery patting the mane of a white pony. She wondered if the child with the neatly combed black curls and the huge brown eyes might be Lord Whitfield. After scrutinizing the painting carefully, she decided it must be his lordship. As he gazed out at her, he appeared confident and filled with mischief. The artist had captured a decided twinkle in his eyes and an impish grin. Just the sort to grow up and throw ribald parties. She snorted, moving on to the bookcase to survey his choice in reading material. It would not surprise her to find lewd French novels in his collection, she mused.

Instead, to her surprise, she found his tastes ran to the classics with a sprinkling of modern novels. She was delighted to see several novels by Maria Edgeworth, the Irish novelist, on his shelves. She found both *Castle Rackrent* and *Belinda*, two of Edgeworth's best and most widely accepted. So, underneath that wild exterior, she decided, Lord Whitfield might not be the savage she had envisioned.

No sooner had she drawn this conclusion than the door flew open and in strolled Lord Whitfield, with Albert trailing behind. He was taller than she had determined from her sitting room window, and far more handsome than she had dreamed. He did not wear the powdered wig so many of the *ton* still preferred. His black hair was pulled back and held by a small band. His dark brown eyes look almost black as his gaze swept over Lila, before he nodded curtly in greeting.

"You wished to speak to me?" His eyes bore into hers and he did not smile. His whole demeanor spoke of his irritation at being inconvenienced.

Perhaps it was his coldness which fired Lila, but she bristled and met his gaze boldly. After curtsying, she replied in a tone as cool as his own, "Yes, I think we should move briskly to the purpose of this visit. I am your closest neighbor and regret that we must meet under such unpleasant circumstances, but this matter simply will not wait." She took a deep breath before plunging ahead. "It is your company, my lord."

"If this is going to take long, Miss Appleby, perhaps we should be seated." He moved over to a plush green sofa and offered her a seat across from him. There still was not one shred of warmth in his voice, and at first

Lila intended to refuse to be seated, but catching the flicker of irritation that swept across his face, she relented and sat in the tall, stuffed chair as ordered. Sitting primly, she placed her hands in her lap and only her occasionally clasping and unclasping them gave away her nervousness.

"Now, you were saying . . ."

"I was discussing the company you keep, Lord Whitfield. I run a school for girls from good homes—a type of finishing school, where the girls learn the finer qualities, such as art, music, a bit of French."

"And what might that have to do with me?" He looked even more perplexed. "Speak up, woman, I haven't all day."

"Mrs. Penkridge was delivering her daughters and Miss Jacinda Kingsbury to my door this morning when you had that . . . that fiasco with some young woman." A deep blush crept up her neck and over her cheeks as she mentioned such a delicate subject.

"Yes, a most unfortunate incident. The young baggage was a thief of the first magnitude, I'm afraid. It just goes to show you what happens, Miss Appleby, when one tries to help strangers." His tone held a double entendre. "Now, Miss Appleby, please try to state your problem. I am a very busy man."

"The problem is that you are ruining my business," she blurted out, and watched for his reaction. Instead of the anger she expected, he merely appeared perplexed.

"I'm sorry, Miss Appleby, but I really don't see the connection. How can I possibly have any effect on your . . . finishing school I believe you call it?"

Lila decided to be honest with him and explain everything that had been troubling her. "Up until you moved into the neighborhood, this was considered a very respectable area." She caught the first flicker of anger in his eyes, but ignored it and continued. "Your late uncle was a model of restraint—"

"I should imagine so, Miss Appleby. He was ninety years old and had been an invalid for the past fifteen years." His tone grew sarcastic. "I don't suppose he did anything you might object to or feel need to criticize."

She jumped up and tried to make amends. "Oh, no, he was a dear old man and my father was great friends with him. I never would dream of besmirching his good name."

"However, you consider me fair game?"

Her cheeks felt hot. He was deliberately skirting the issue and trying to make her look bad. "I am going to be blunt with you, Lord Whitfield. Your conduct this morning with the lady of questionable reputation was deplorable. The Penkridge sisters' mother witnessed the whole sorry debacle. She has informed me that if the goings-on over here continue, she will remove her daughters from my school. I can not afford for this to happen. I am running a wonderful school, and I will not let the likes of you spoil it for me." There! She had risen to the occasion and spoken her mind. Instead of being angry as she'd expected, Lord Whitfield appeared amused.

He clapped. "Bravo! What spunk! Spoken like a true bluestocking!"

Now he moved menacingly close and glared down

at her. "Miss Appleby, I am from northern England, and I know we may be a tad more barbaric there than you refined social arbiters from London, however, let me remind you of one of the oldest of English laws: a man's home is his castle. If I wish to cavort on my lawn with"—he gestured wildly—"with a band of roving gypsies, then I shall do so with no regard as to my neighbors' reaction."

"Then you won't change your conduct?" she gasped. She had anticipated meekness, embarrassment, even a noble apology, but never this ungentlemanly refusal to cooperate.

"Indeed not!" He glanced at the porcelain clock on the mantle and said, "Now if you'll excuse me, I have other more important matters to attend to."

"If my father were alive, he'd call you out to a duel for such conduct," she stammered, appalled at his lack of sensitivity to her position.

"I don't suppose you'd be interested in taking his place?" he retorted with a grin.

He didn't even take her seriously. She stared in stunned silence, watching as a smile crossed his handsome features, and in spite of herself, she noticed how his eyes crinkled at the corners when he grinned. He was an outrageous flirt!

"Or perhaps you'd prefer to bargain for a kiss." He stepped closer, and she was forced to retreat two steps backward, still staring up at him mutely. "Let's see." He put his finger on her cheek and ran it lightly from cheekbone to chin, teasingly. "For a kiss I'd bring my paramour, as I'm sure you think the little baggage to be, to the side entrance instead of the front. How would that be, eh?" His dark brown eyes twinkled seductively.

Lila pushed his finger aside, although her heart was racing from his touch and she was having difficulty thinking straight. She cleared her throat and stammered, "You are a devil, sir! You'll never have your way with me, I can assure you!"

"Hmmm, we'll see," he replied rakishly. His eyes swept over her with such arrogance that she blushed anew, feeling as though he could see through her cape and gown.

She turned and fled the room, his laughter echoing after her. As she slammed the front door, she muttered over her shoulder to a very perplexed Albert, who stood outside polishing the brass knocker, "I'll rid London of this uncouth barbarian or I'm not an Appleby!"

Without further ado, she lifted her skirts and stomped off down the front walk, slamming the iron gate with a loud bang.

The gall of the infernal man, she stewed as she marched down the sidewalk and up to her own front door. Never had she encountered such a roguish person. The thing that annoyed her the most was that she had trembled at his touch when he ran his finger down her cheek. Even now she could feel where his warm hand had touched her soft flesh. The man was a devil for sure, and she'd never succumb to his charms. Never!

Now she had to set her plan into action. She intended to rid London of the likes of his lordship!

* * *

"At last you're back," gasped Maude when she heard the front door slam. She was standing in the foyer where she had been pacing the floor and worrying. "What happened? You look positively distraught. Did he throw you out? I knew I should have gone with you."

"I wish he had laid a hand on me. I'd have run him through with a fire poker." Still angry, Lila whipped off her bonnet and jammed it on the wooden peg. She paced the floor as she unbuttoned the fasteners on her cape, angry, frustrated and upset with herself for feeling so helpless in Whitfield's company. While she wanted to be rid of him on the one hand, on the other she admired his ability to throw caution to the wind and live his life with fun and abandon, something she'd never had the luxury of doing. However, she had no intention allowing him to ruin the one source of income she had available to her. Heat rose in her cheeks again at the thought of how indifferent to her plight he had been.

"My, my, love, you are agitated. Here, come into the library and let's talk," Maude whispered, and glanced around, fearing Hortense might hear her. At times she'd suspected the girl of eavesdropping. "The girls have finished their music lesson, and I've put them to work on their French assignment." She bustled ahead of her niece, opening the library door and waiting patiently for Lila to hang up her cape and wrap a worn cashmere shawl around her shoulders before she followed.

"Have you noticed how dense poor Jacinda is? Carries the worst tune I've ever heard, sings like a washboard rubbing against the pot, and the poor thing can't conjugate the first French verb."

"Auntie, as pretty as she is and as large as her dowry, it will never matter whether she can read a word of French or not. She's bubbly, not to mention a tad wild, and she will snare some young swain before the Season well begins. And believe me, he'll never miss her singing or French talents." She laughed and grinned at her aunt. "Should my problems be as small as hers." Lila moved to the nearest leather chair and collapsed into it. "I have never had an experience like the one I just went through."

"Good heavens, dear. The man didn't accost you, did he?"

"No." She wasn't ready to tell about the threat of a kiss. "But the odious man didn't take my problem seriously." She looked her aunt in the eye and said through clenched teeth, "I can tell you one thing though, he's no gentleman. I'd as soon take my chances with a gutter snipe as with that nob!" She grew angrier and jumped up to walk off some of her pent-up energy. "You'd think he'd have some honor."

"I didn't know his honor was in question," replied Maude, not at all sure what had really taken place next door. Lila was acting very strange and her cheeks were flushed. "He didn't try to ravish you, did he?" This was not a topic she felt comfortable discussing with her niece, yet she knew it had to be mentioned.

Finally Lila decided to confide in her aunt. "He offered to exchange a kiss for the discretion of using the side entrance rather than the front when he brings home his . . . his trollops."

Maude gasped and fanned herself furiously, as she always did whenever she was upset, regardless of the temperature. "He didn't! If your father were alive he'd go over there and horsewhip him."

Shaking her head, Lila frowned. "No, knowing our Lord Whitfield, he'd charm Father into having a drink, and the two would come staggering over here arm in arm and well in their cups." She looked her aunt straight in the eye. "No, the man is a devil. He can charm the likes of most, but he'll never get around me. I'll have him driven out of London in disgrace if he doesn't have a care."

"And just how do you expect to accomplish this feat?"

Lila shrugged, dropped back down in her chair, and stared at the grate where the coals of the morning's fire smoldered and glowed a bright red. She conjured up all kinds of revenges for the mighty Lord Whitfield while she stewed. "There has to be a way, Aunt Maude." She looked over at her aunt with a deter- mined glint in her eyes. Her face brightened and she grinned. "This is war, dear aunt. I have a plan that will bring the mighty Lord Whitfield to his knees."

Chapter 3

LORD WHITFIELD AROSE from his bed in late afternoon, proceeded to dress quickly, then sauntered downstairs to await his good friend and carousing companion, the Earl of Leyton.

Life in London was beginning to bore Whitfield, and he sat in his study staring at the fire, mulling over possible adventures he and Haydon might find amusing, while he waited for his friend to arrive. At Blyton Castle in Leicester there were many things one might do for pleasure. There was hunting, a sport he enjoyed greatly, and fishing in his well-stocked streams, plus horse racing in all its various forms. He sighed deeply and stretched his long legs restlessly as he thought of the wonders of home.

Whitfield had been to London many times since he came of age, but always knowing that he might return to Leicester. The whirl of parties, dances, soirées, and crushes were exciting at first, but he supposed he was growing jaded; the constant stream of beauties no longer held much interest for him. He still enjoyed the pursuit of a beautiful woman, but once she was captured, most often she turned into a very dull creature without an intelligent thought in her head. Not at all like that dreadful Miss Appleby next door, who actually had a spark in her eye and a backbone to match. His charms hadn't meant a whit to her.

What was her first name—Lily? Laureen?—something that started with an L. He pondered the matter while he stared at the fire smoldering in the grate, his fingers arched under his chin as he tapped an index finger absentmindedly. The name wouldn't come to him. It kept slipping from his grasp.

Standing up, he stretched his six-foot frame and strolled over to the grate, punching at the fire until it blazed up once more. Lila! Lila Appleby! That's what she had said. Yes, the name Lila suited her.

The maidenly Miss Appleby thought him a bit of a savage. Of that he was certain, but what could she possibly know of his true feelings? He tried to dismiss her opinion of him, still he was not accustomed to being looked upon with such haughty and vivid disregard. The woman could not abide him.

Whitfield tried to recall her appearance, but all he remembered was that she was tall, slender, and reminded him of a brown bird dressed in that plain cape and feathered hat that looked like it had molted. He shook his head to clear it. What was the matter with him, wasting time thinking of such woman? Yet there had been a spark about her. Those blue eyes had met his, fiercely defying him to challenge her remarks.

Why she had as good as called him a barbarian and would have no part of being bullied by him. He smiled as he remembered how she had not even flinched when he'd taunted her with the threat of a kiss. He wondered what her lips might have felt like, had he carried it out.

At that moment he heard a commotion in the hallway that brought him abruptly out of his daydream. In strode his good friend, Haydon.

"So, how's the hangover, old chap?" asked Haydon in greeting as he crossed over to the chair across from Whitfield, and plopped onto it. "I feel worse than a man who has been run over by a carriage and six horses."

"I'm fine," replied Whitfield. "I really haven't given much thought to my headache, as my day has been so busy." Crossing his legs, which strained the fabric of his tight-fitting trousers to the point of bursting, he continued. "I had a most annoying visitor this morning. A Miss Appleby from next door, who said that I was giving the neighborhood a bad name with my cavorting and such nonsense. A true prude if one ever existed. Ruined my morning's sleep and was a devilish bother." He paused for a moment. "Do you know anything about her, by any chance? I thought living in London the year round you might have had an opportunity to cross paths with her."

"Appleby, you say?" Haydon concentrated on the name for a few minutes. "The name does ring a bell, but I don't think it's the young woman I know. I think it was her father, the late Alexander Appleby with whom I'm acquainted. The man was quite the gambler.

Would wager on anything. I remember once he bet on which leaf next would fall from a tree outside the Ram's Horn Pub." Haydon shook his head and chuckled. "Likeable chap. A bit too partial to the sauce, but a great sportsman, by Jove. Come to think of it, he died owing me a vowel. Took his paper after a fierce night of cards at Brooks's last winter."

Whitfield's interest perked up. "You hold a note on the man?"

"Well, of course I'd never call it in, you understand. Merely a few hundred pounds, and from what I've heard since, he left his only daughter in rather destitute circumstances."

"I'll buy that vowel from you, Haydon. You don't have it on you by any chance, do you?"

"As a matter of fact, I do. Think it's right here in my wallet. Give me a minute and I'll check for you." Haydon fumbled through his breast pocket until he found his brown leather wallet and withdrew it. After searching through a sheaf of papers, he chuckled. "Here's Daphne Wilcox's address. I'd forgotten about her. Wonder how she enjoys being the mistress of Stonehouse now that she's married to the old earl?"

"Not as well as she enjoyed being your mistress, I'm certain, you rascal. She's probably still raving over the way you treated her." Growing impatient, Whitfield leaned closer. "Have you found it yet?"

"Ah, here it is. Yes, five hundred pounds." He nodded. "Poor chap simply couldn't win that night. We all tried to get him to throw in his cards and call it a night, but no one could persuade him." Haydon handed the piece of paper over to Whitfield. "I can't imagine why you'd want it, but you can have it."

"No, I want to buy this from you." Whitfield placed the pound notes in his friend's hand. "This may come in handy later, should our Miss Appleby continue to make a nuisance of herself."

Haydon eyed his friend suspiciously. "What are you up to? You aren't thinking of going over and dunning the poor woman or evicting her from her home, by any chance? I must say, old chap, as one friend to another, that would be a most ungentlemanly way to be rid of a nuisance."

Whitfield shook his head. "No, but if she gives me too much trouble, I can always flaunt the debt in her face and—"

"She'll slink home like a bitten cur?" Haydon frowned. "This doesn't sound like you, Whitfield."

Whitfield laughed and shook his head. "Somehow I can't picture Miss Lila Appleby slinking home, even in defeat. No, I'd say she'd retreat like a raging bull."

"Well, where shall we go this afternoon? Do you desire another evening the likes of last?" Haydon shifted his weight in his chair and held a well-booted foot up to the fire. "You know, friend, that we need to be settling down to a nice wife who'd keep us straight and out of such places as the Alley Cat, where one night we both are going to find a knife driven through our shoulder blades."

"Nonsense. You aren't growing old on me are you?"

"No, to the contrary, but I must admit that the conquest isn't the sport it once was. Do you ever feel that way?"

"Yes, and when I do, I take myself a new mistress. Now come along, Haydon." Lord Whitfield stood and rang for the butler. "We'll get our wraps from Albert and be off. I thought tonight we might stop by Lady Lamb's for drinks, move on to Swann's for a late meal, and then look in at White's. I feel lucky tonight."

"What? No plans to meet up with any ladies this evening? Was last night too much for you?"

"That little piece of baggage was drunk and followed me home. I had no intention sleeping with her," snapped Lord Whitfield. "To make matters worse, she was a thief of the first order and tried to make off with her weight in silver from this place." Remembering the scene Miss Appleby had witnessed and feeling slightly embarrassed over the spectacle he had made of himself annoyed him even more. "There was a most distasteful foray in the front yard, which I'm afraid was witnessed by Miss Appleby, who marched over afterwards to chastise me."

Haydon lifted an eyebrow and studied his friend closely. They had been the best of friends for years, and he recognized the change in Whitfield. Miss Appleby's visit had touched a nerve in Whitfield. Still, he knew it best to remain silent.

They moved on into the foyer where Albert waited with their cloaks. "Do you wish your carriage, sir?"

"No, I think the spring air will do us both good, Albert. We'll walk and if we tire, I'll hail a hackney."

The two gentlemen stepped out into the cool spring air of late afternoon and started down the sidewalk. To Whitfield's consternation, who should appear from around the corner but Miss Appleby and an elderly lady. There was nothing to do but continue on his way.

Lila and her aunt had been to Mr. Matlock's pawn shop and were returning with the little money left after the butcher had been paid part of his bill and was satisfied for the time being. The pound notes left were safely tucked in her reticule, and Lila's spirits were quite cheerful until she spotted Whitfield. "Aunt Maude, here comes that odious Lord Whitfield. What shall we do?" she whispered frantically, feeling her heart flutter foolishly.

"Why, continue down the sidewalk, love. This is a free city, you know."

"I know that, but I don't want to pass him."

"Unless you give him an obvious snub, Lila, there's no other choice." She took the girl firmly by the elbow and guided her forward. "We'll simply nod in greeting should he look our way and move swiftly along." Eyeing Lila out of the corner of her eye, she remarked, "I don't think that blush rising to your cheeks is going to be missed by him, however. Haven't see a man do that to you in years. Most pleasant change, I might add."

"Aunt Maude, don't you dare chide me right now. Oh, here he comes. For a moment I saw him hesitate and thought he might change course and go away." She gritted her teeth. "A gentleman would have done that! He's a monster!"

"A very handsome one, my dear. Now if he speaks, nod politely. We are neighbors, and it never hurts to be polite. I must say, that young man with him is a handsome one, too. Who do you suppose he is?"

"I haven't the slightest idea, but if he's with the likes

of Whitfield, he's an unprincipled dandy, I'm sure." Lila walked on, ramrod straight, trying to look anywhere other than at the approaching men.

When the gentlemen reached the ladies, Lord Whitfield tipped his hand and said, "Good afternoon, Miss Appleby."

Lila nodded a curt greeting and tilted her head skyward, picking up her pace until Maude had to almost run to keep up with her.

"My goodness, Lila. You certainly snubbed Lord Whitfield." She touched Lila on her arm. "And slow down, I'm winded already. Whatever has gotten into you?"

"I'm sorry, but I don't want to get involved with the likes of them. There's no telling what Lord Whitfield might have said." She did slow her pace though, allowing her aunt to catch up. "I tell you, Aunt Maude, he is a rake of most notorious sort."

"That may be true, but he's handsome and single, and it never hurts for you to keep that in mind."

"Humph!" replied Lila.

When Lila and her aunt were out of earshot, Haydon turned to his friend and said, "She is certainly an aloof person. I've received warmer greeting from cuckold husbands."

Whitfield laughed, but then set his jaw in a decisive manner. "That woman is downright insulting. If she thinks I'm as odious as a leper, then perhaps we should give her reason to feel that way."

"And how, pray, do you intend to accomplish this feat?" Whitfield didn't answer immediately, and they strolled on down the street in silence.

Suddenly Whitfield snapped his fingers and stopped, turning to his friend, a wide grin spread across his face. "I have the perfect way to infuriate my good neighbor. She'll be seething or I miss my guess." He chuckled at the thought of what he planned. "Uncle left each of his most loyal staff a token gift of a few pounds and those in his employ for many years up to five hundred pounds. The estate is settled to the point that I can give out these bequeaths now. I had planned to wait until later in the summer, however I think I'll have a picnic on the grounds and at the end of the party I'll give out their gifts. I'll put Bennie, the stable boy, in charge of the affair; he's a wild lad and will know how to produce a fun affair for them. He can order all the food and grog they please. They've earned it." Whitfield placed his finger to his cheek and thought for a moment. "Let's have the event three days from now, and I'll let the staff invite their families."

Haydon studied his friend suspiciously. "What's the point?"

"We'll also invite the mighty Miss Appleby's staff since they often helped out over here in the past. Should we include Miss Appleby and her aunt?" Whitfield was warming to the idea, realizing how much it would irritate the haughty Miss Appleby. He grinned to himself at his cleverness.

"From the way she behaved a moment ago, I don't think she'd consider accepting the invitation if the Prince Regent were to be the guest of honor. And you certainly don't want to mix the aristocracy with the hired help. Besides the staff's spirits will be dampened if we lurk around. If this is to be their party, then you shouldn't even appear until near the end, and then only long enough to give out the gifts."

Whitfield thought about this for a moment and then nodded. "You're probably correct. In that case, let's have a lawn party and give her a show she won't forget."

"Aren't you being a bit rash, Whitfield? She did appear to be a lady, and some of the staff's associates are a bit unsavory." Haydon eyed his friend suspiciously. "The loud noise is bound to offend your Miss Appleby's delicate sensibilities. And you did mention she's running a school for young ladies. I've seen one, a gorgeous redhead, coming to and from the house or riding in her carriage several times lately. In fact, I'd like to meet her one day. We'd do well to patronize your Miss Appleby to meet the redhead." Seeing that he was making no headway with Whitfield, Haydon shook his head. "Are you certain about this? It's rather a rash gesture to entertain one's staff on the side lawn."

Whitfield grinned and looked at his friend with the gleam of devilment in his eyes that Haydon knew signaled Whitfield was about to stir up mischief. "If I'm going to be branded a blackguard, then by heavens, I'll act like one."

Chapter 4

"Take your lecherous hands off me!" A young girl's laughter drifted through Lila's parlor window as she struggled to continue her class, determined to ignore the noise created by the party next door. Lila finished instructing the girls in a lesson on writing gracious thank you notes.

"Give an old man a kiss!" yelled another reveler. The girls giggled and Lila's face turned crimson before she regained her composure.

"Miss Appleby, what's going on next door?" asked Jacinda politely, looking the picture of innocence. This sent the Penkridge girls into new peals of laughter.

"Young lady, never mind. I want all of you to take out your French lesson books. We'll begin the conjugation of verbs with . . . with . . ." Lila gulped, for the next verb was "love." "With *aimer*, to be followed by *manger*, *dormir*—"

"A week's free ale for a kiss!" a lusty voice called out

49

as the sounds of revelry continued to drift through the window.

"For you love, I'll kiss ye fer free!" a female voice shouted back.

"That does it," snapped Lila, shutting her textbook with a sound thud. She was so angry she feared she'd burst into tears in front of the girls. The nerve of Lord Whitfield to do this to her! "You girls may go to the piano and play lively waltzes until your carriages arrive."

"But if we play, Miss Appleby, we won't be able to hear what's happening next door," said Idelia Penkridge in her most innocent voice, although she cast a mischievous glance toward her sister.

"That's precisely the point, Idelia. Now do as I say and play and sing until your carriage arrives. It should be here within the hour. You've done enough work today in any case."

"What are you planning to do about the party going on next door? Are you going to try and stop it?" Jacinda went to the window and pulled back the curtain.

"Jacinda Kingsbury, you come away from that window this instant! I'll not have one of my girls seen by that drunken band of revelers next door." Lila knew she was saying too much and that the Penkridges would report every oath, every vile word, and perhaps even a few extras to their mother the moment they reached home. She was so angry with Lord Whitfield that had she a horsewhip at that moment, she'd march over and apply it to his backside personally.

The party next door had been raging for the past

hour and continued to grow louder by the minute. She had seen the people arriving right after she and the girls had finished luncheon, and the unease had begun to creep through her body, for the people entering Whitfield's gate were of the most common sort. He must have gone into the Black Pirate and invited everybody there. And the spirits that flowed next door made her shudder. Everyone seemed to be holding a pint tankard, and from the increase in the volume of noise, she suspected the barrels were filled with liquor of the strongest sort.

What had provoked Lord Whitfield to entertain a yard full of thugs, thieves and, clearly, women of the evening? At first when the invitation had arrived for her staff she had thought it a noble gesture and even, for only the briefest of moments, felt a pang of remorse for her low opinion of Lord Whitfield. But now, with the party in full swing, it had turned into a scandal.

And the smirk she'd seen on Lord Whitfield's face the one time she'd ventured out on her porch was the outside of enough. He'd been strolling down his sidewalk and had actually had the audacity to tip his hat to her and blow her a kiss. A kiss! How odious!

Finally, her nerves were so wrought that she had to get out of the house and away from the unsightly behavior. She clapped her hands to gain the girls' attention. They stopped immediately and turned to stare at her, all innocence, as though they were not acutely aware of her agitation over the events taking place next door.

"Girls, girls! Get your wraps. I have decided the weather is so lovely today that I can't keep you cooped up in this house another minute. We'll go for a nature walk in the direction of your carriages, and I'll dismiss class when they arrive." She smiled at them as they let out a cheer. "You do sound excited over the event. Now hurry and do as I say."

The girls scurried to gather their belongings. Wraps were on and bonnets tied pertly to the side of chins within minutes. Soon they were out the door, giggling and chattering.

Jacinda cupped her hand over her mouth. "Let's sneak a look through the bushes when we pass," she whispered to the Penkridge sisters as they hurried down the stone front steps.

Sensing their unusual slowness, Lila snapped briskly, "Come along, girls! Quickly! Quickly! We don't want to be accosted by anyone next door."

They marched obediently past the iron fence surrounding Whitfield's yard, trying to glimpse some of the goings-on taking place on his side lawn.

The giggling girls, led by Lila, whose bonnet was turned up not a whit more than her nose, strode briskly by the earl's lawn party as screeches of laughter and hearty guffaws drifted toward them.

It was a beautiful spring afternoon and the flowering shrubs and jonquils added such color to the lawns that Lila's spirits soared in spite of herself. She loved the clean smell of new-cut grass and budding sweetgum trees.

She began to relax and enjoy their excursion. The girls were behaving nicely and spending their time trying to name as many flowers and trees as possible. Lila thought she had saved the situation, when to her shock, who did she see strolling down the street toward her but the devil himself accompanied by another man. Lila recognized the blond man as one whom she had seen enter and leave the Whitfield home on many occasions.

Lila and the girls were too near to turn away, so there was nothing to do but brave the encounter.

"Good afternoon, Miss Appleby," said Lord Whitfield, tipping his tall hat. "It's a lovely day for a stroll, isn't it?" His eyes scanned the giggling girls at her side. "But the weather cannot hold a candle to the beauty of these charming ladies who accompany you." He bowed graciously to the girls.

Turning, Whitfield added, "And please let me introduce my good friend, Lord Robert Haydon, Earl of Leyton."

Haydon whipped off his hat and bowed deeply. "I have wanted so long to meet your charming students—they are students are they not, Miss Appleby?"

There was no polite alternative for Lila; she had to introduce the girls, although she would rather have introduced them to a hated bondsman who would sell them into the slave trade than to make even this slight a concession.

"The Penkridge sisters, Hortense and Idelia." The girls curtsied clumsily, struggling to control their urge to giggle. Hortense even batted her eyelashes coquettishly, and Lila felt the urge to shake the silly chit.

"And who might this pretty one be, with her flaming red hair that is enough to quicken any man's heart?" asked Haydon, clearly taken by Jacinda's beauty.

"Miss Jacinda Kingsbury, the daughter of Mr. Malcolm Kingsbury. You may have met her father. He is president of the King's Bank on Brompton Road in Knightsbridge."

"Of course, I have met her father many times, but I can assure you this is my first meeting of Miss Kingsbury. I'd never forget a face as lovely as hers." Robert said this to Lila, but his eyes never left Jacinda, nor did hers him. He took her hand and kissed it, bowing deeply again. "While this is our first meeting, Miss Kingsbury, I do hope we have the opportunity to meet again soon."

"Perhaps you can come for tea one afternoon, if it's all right with Miss Appleby," said Jacinda, still gazing at Lord Haydon.

"Oh, please come, sir," chimed in Hortense. "We've so been looking forward to practicing our skills as hostesses."

Lila wanted to pinch Jacinda soundly, but she could say nothing other than, "That's a lovely idea, Jacinda, however I'm sure Lord Haydon has more pressing issues at hand than having tea with a group of school girls and their teacher."

"Nonsense, I'd be delighted to accept." Haydon finally forced himself to look away from Jacinda and smile at the other girls.

This left no alternative but for Lila to include Lord Whitfield too, so she turned to him and in the coolest of voices said, "Lord Whitfield, we'd be most happy to have you join us also."

"What a splendid idea," chirped Hortense, giving Lord Whitfield her most charming smile and fluttering her eyelashes again. She reminded Lila of someone who'd gotten a cinder in her eye.

For a few seconds Lord Whitfield remained silent, and the briefest of frowns flickered across his forehead before he answered. Lila thought he was about to decline. She felt a moment of elation at not having to be in the same room with him, but at the same time, a twinge of disappointment which baffled her. What was there about this man that intrigued her?

Jacinda placed her hand on Whitfield's arm and looked up at him with her most provocative smile. "My lord, you must come too. Our party wouldn't be complete without the pleasure of your company and conversation."

"Then it's settled. I would be happy to accept." He smiled and bowed graciously, his black beaver hat almost scraping the pavement. "No one other than a heartless ogre could resist such a charming invitation as yours, Miss Kingsbury."

"Would Thursday at two be agreeable then?" asked Lila, already feeling her heart race. The roar in her ears made Lord Whitfield's acceptance almost inaudible. She couldn't believe she was inviting him to her home.

Once the final arrangements were settled, the gentlemen bowed graciously and took their leave.

The girls and Lila moved off briskly down the street. By now Lila was so nervous there was a queasy feeling in her stomach. How could she ever get ready to entertain Whitfield in the short time she had? Already her mind raced ahead, and she thought of polishing silver, Cook baking her tiny fruit pies dusted with sugar. She even began worrying over the sad appearance of her parlor. It would not take Lord Whitfield long to realize what dire circumstances she was in. Oh, how had she allowed Jacinda to put her in such a predicament? When the moment was right, she'd scold Jacinda for taking such a liberty.

However, she had to concede that one good thing had come out of the debacle. The girls were so excited over meeting two peers whom she felt confident both sets of parents would approve. How often did trades-men's daughters get the opportunity to share tea with an earl? And two at once were more than many mamas could pray for.

The rest of the walk passed quickly as the girls were all atwitter over what to wear on Thursday. It was fi-nally decided that each would bring an afternoon dress when they came to school on Thursday morning and then change for the very important tea.

And, Lila had to concede, it was excellent training for the girls to entertain such prominent guests. Maude would be delighted to help her plan. She had been af-ter Lila for months to start entertaining again. It might be fun to enjoy oneself again, thought Lila, even if Lord Whitfield did have to be her first guest. And he cer-tainly had no idea how much animosity she held to-ward him for his garden party. Why wasn't he there himself, she wondered irritably. But even her annoy-ance didn't stop her feeling a strange flutter of excite-ment over his coming to tea.

The girls' carriages arrived shortly afterward, and they seemed sad to be leaving Lila's company for the first time since classes began.

"Can't we give you a ride home, Miss Appleby?"

asked Hortense as she stepped into the Penkridge carriage. "We have so many things to discuss yet that I hate to leave you."

"Please do ride with us," chimed in Idelia.

Lila shook her head. "That is most kind of you to offer, however, I'd like to walk a while longer. This spring air is to my liking, and I need to clear my mind." She glanced at the girls and smiled. "There is so much to do before Thursday that it makes my head whirl."

The coachman closed the carriage door and moved back to await Hortense's orders.

"Good day then," said Hortense. "Oh, Miss Appleby I can't wait to tell Mama everything that's happened today."

"It might be wise not to mention Lord Whitfield's party. What do you think, Miss Appleby?" asked Idelia.

"I don't want you girls keeping secrets from your mother, however, we don't want to upset her. It would be disastrous if she refused you permission to have tea with Lord Whitfield and Lord Haydon."

"I quite agree," said Hortense. She signaled for the driver to be off. "Goodbye, dear teacher!"

Lila smiled as she turned toward home herself. The girls waved excitedly until their carriages were out of sight. This brought a much needed smile to Lila's face. She had feared the girls were not happy at her school. Now all she had to do was worry about the upcoming tea.

Chapter 5

ONCE THE GIRLS were on their way, Lila changed her mind and decided to walk on to Knightsbridge and purchased some new ribbon for her jonquil gown. Perhaps Aunt Maude would be able to bring the jonquil up to scratch or at least freshen it up a bit with some new bows. She reached into her reticule to count out the precious coins to be sure she could afford such a luxury.

The trip took longer than she had anticipated. It was a lovely spring afternoon with the slightest of breezes blowing, and she soon found herself walking idly by the many shop windows gazing at the newest of fabrics and laces. How grand it must be to be able to stroll into a shop and purchase ivory combs and silver hair fasteners. She sighed wistfully as she moved gracefully down the street.

When she did notice the time, the sun was moving

rapidly toward the horizon and she stepped up her pace.

As she walked home, she became aware of two dirty, poorly dressed men who fell into step behind her. An uneasy sense stirred in her immediately. She even debated hailing a carriage, but then scolded herself for even thinking of such a frivolous waste of her few precious pounds. Instead she quickened her step, glancing at the lamplighters, relieved to see them beginning to make their rounds. She realized she had been foolish to make the long trip so late in the day. Still, there was nothing to do now but move swiftly along.

Walking rapidly, she soon left the business district of Knightsbridge behind her and started through the residential area, passing the many townhouses where on most afternoons people would be coming or leaving. But because of the late hour, most were home, dressing for their evening's entertainment. Not even a servant scurried down the street. By this time, the men's footsteps were beginning to frighten her, because it was evident the men did not belong in this neighborhood.

She turned another corner and drew a deep breath, for home was now only a few blocks away. Suddenly she heard the men quicken their pace. Lila glanced furtively over her shoulder convinced now that the two men were indeed following her and meant to harm her. She swallowed hard, trying to moisten her throat, which had gone dry with fear as the alarm rose in her. Straining, she scanned the street hoping to see a friendly face, but because of the hour all seemed to be indoors taking tea or their evening meal. Aunt Maude would be frantic by now.

Her first instinct was to clutch her package of ribbon close to her side and to walk faster, but every time she quickened her pace, so did they.

She had just turned the third corner when one of the men came up to her and bumped her hard, throwing her off balance. She threw out her hands to break her fall and the other man snatched her reticule and the package of ribbon. "No! Stop!" she cried helplessly, her voice rising in anger.

Suddenly she heard the loud sound of approaching horses and a shout rang out: "Halt where you are!"

She struggled to her feet, brushing off her gown and wiping her hands as she looked around to see where the sounds were coming from.

Relief filled her eyes as she recognized Lord Whitfield, who leaped from his carriage and shouted to his driver. Both men had witnessed the robbery, so the driver set off after the thieves while Whitfield ran to her aid.

"Are you hurt, Miss Appleby?" Whitfield took her arm and helped her to a nearby bench. "Let me have a look at your hands."

Lila could not stop their trembling as she obeyed. Hugh pulled out a white linen handkerchief and began brushing the grit and dirt from her upturned palms. She made no effort to pull away as he gently cleaned them.

"They took my reticule. I'm so glad you came along." She looked up at him, and it was the first time she had ever favored him with a truly friendly smile.

"Are you all right? I saw the whole thing, but my driver couldn't get here before they attacked you. I'm so sorry; we did our best." Whitfield sat down beside Lila and put his arm around her, patting her shoulder reassuringly. "There, there, you're fine now. Please don't cry, Miss Appleby."

"I'm so ashamed, but I c-ca-can't stop myself. It frightened me so much." Large tears spilled down her cheeks and when he drew her closer, comforting her, she finally gave way to her desire to lay her head on his shoulder and rest in the safety of his arms. Had she not been in shock, she never would have been so bold as to do such a thing, but at the moment he was as comforting as her father.

"Did they get much money?" Lord Whitfield held her closer, beginning to enjoy her warmth. To his surprise he discovered she was far more attractive, now that her hair had fallen out of its tight knot and tiny wisps curled fetchingly around her temples.

Once Lila began to calm down and stop trembling, she grew aware of her disheveled appearance, and she also grew acutely aware of her closeness to the earl. Whitfield continued to rub her arm and hold her hand safely in his.

She wiped at her eyes once more and pulled out of his grasp. "I must look a fright. My hair is in a shambles." She patted at it and blushed deeply.

"To the contrary, Miss Appleby. You have lovely hair, and it is most becoming in that fashion."

She giggled nervously, still not fully in control of her emotions. "What an odd way to get a new hair style, don't you think?" She looked around for her hairpins, but didn't see them, so she finally gave up and let her hair fall free once more, and it cascaded around her shoulders. "What happened to my bonnet?"

Lord Whitfield walked over to the hedge and looked behind it. He lifted out a crushed velvet bonnet with a few sprigs of roses left on its brim. "I'm afraid it's the worse for wear. You seem to have broken a ribbon when your head struck the iron fence. Thank goodness you didn't scar that lovely face. You do realize, Miss Appleby, that you're a very fortunate young lady. What were you doing out here alone this time of day, anyhow?" His voice held a scolding tone.

"I decided to stop by the ribbon shop for a few minutes, and I'm afraid I let the time get away from me."

"Here's 'er purse, sir. And I believe this 'ere's the package she was carrying too, but I ain't sure." The coachman handed his finds to Whitfield. "I'm afraid, sir, that the men got away. I almost had them when they tossed these items and I stopped to retrieve them from the gutter. When I looked up again, they were 'alfway down the next turn."

"That's all right, Sid. You did a good job in recovering Miss Appleby's possessions." Whitfield turned to Lila. "This is your reticule, isn't it?"

"Oh, yes, and my package too. I am ever so grateful to both of you for all your help. Now I really must be getting on home, as night has caught us now."

"Nonsense, I'll not hear of you walking the rest of the way alone. Please get in my carriage, and I'll take you home."

"But, sir, you were on your way somewhere, and

I've been enough bother to you." She stood on shaky legs.

"Miss Appleby, you are the most exasperating creature. I am not going to stand here and argue with you. Do as I say." Whitfield took her arm and helped her into his carriage. He had never known a woman as stubborn and headstrong as she.

Lila rode along with Lord Whitfield in silence, swaying with the motion of the carriage, listening to the horses' hooves on the cobbled street. She still was too shaken by all that had happened to think clearly, and the suddenness of being thrown together with her most unpleasant neighbor left her speechless. As they rode through the city in the twilight, she felt grateful that her face was hidden in the shadows. As she thought back over the assault, she remembered placing her head on Lord Whitfield's shoulder—had she actually done such a brazen thing? Yes, her mind was clear on the matter, and she rubbed her hands together nervously. They were cut and scraped, and she gave a small cry of pain.

Lord Whitfield moved to her side instantly. "Are you hurt, Miss Appleby? Is a bone broken?"

"No, I just forgot how sore my hands are, and I clasped them together rather roughly. It's truly nothing, my lord."

"Here. I'll turn the carriage around and take you by the doctor's house. We'll let him have a look at you."

"Oh, no!" Lila panicked at the thought of the expense of a doctor's bill. The mere thought frightened her almost as much as the theft. "I'm fine. Please, take me home. Aunt Maude will be frantic if I don't arrive soon. She didn't even know I was going on into Knightsbridge. I left intending only to walk the girls to meet their carriages, and she has no idea where I am."

"As you wish." He settled back on the seat and made no further comment.

They rode on in silence once more. Lila simply couldn't think of a thing to converse with him about, and she was so exhausted that she really didn't care if he found her less than sociable. Better silence than silly prattle had always been her motto.

When they passed under a lamplight Lila studied Lord Whitfield curiously from between half-opened eyes. She didn't want him to catch her staring. He wore a black frock coat with frog hooks and tall black leather boots that came to the knees. It was evident he was on his way out for an evening of amusement.

"I hope I'm not delaying you," she said, when she realized she might be making him late for a social event. "I feel terrible putting you out this way."

"I have time to help a lady in distress," he replied noncommittally.

At last they pulled up in front of her house and the door opened immediately. Maude's silhouette filled the doorway and Lila's spirits soared. She would not have to talk to Lord Whitfield alone.

Whitfield stepped out of the carriage and held out his hand to her. There was nothing for her to do but place hers in his large, strong hand.

"You don't have to see me to the door," she stammered. "I wish to thank you again for every . . . everything."

"It was my pleasure." He bowed gracefully and kissed her hand lightly. To her amazement, his soft lips on her outstretched hand sent a small current through her. Turning quickly, she dashed up the steps, not waiting for his carriage to pull away.

Chapter 6

FOR THE NEXT two days all the Appleby household was adither with preparations for the visit of the two earls. The girls spent every minute Lila allowed discussing Lord Whitfield and Lord Haydon, deciding who liked which gentleman more. Jacinda staked her claim on Lord Haydon and Hortense quickly agreed to set her cap for Lord Whitfield. Instead of being pleased for the girls, Lila found herself being slightly irritated by the entire business.

"I tell you, Aunt Maude, I'm not certain this is a wise decision," Lila said while she and her aunt were polishing the last of the family silver. "Thank heavens I didn't sell this." She giggled, holding up the tea pot and rubbing an especially difficult place. "I wavered between it and the punch bowl for some time the other day."

"You ought not be doing away with your mother's favorite pieces, Lila. I don't think it's wise."

"It may not be wise, but it's definitely necessary. That punch bowl brought enough to feed the household for a month, plus enough left over to buy sweets for tomorrow's tea." Lila placed the teapot on the table and moved on to the creamer. "I do have to admit the girls have shown a new interest in deportment and etiquette since learning such important guests are coming." She laughed. "Even Mrs. Penkridge sent a note congratulating me on having such splendid visitors."

"One day Lord Whitfield's a scoundrel, and the next he's a special guest." Maude chuckled and wiped at a smudge on her cheek.

"You know why she's so enthusiastic; she thinks he'd be a wonderful match for Hortense. She's even ordered an entire new outfit for the girl to wear tomorrow. Madame Monteil has put two of her seamstresses to work on the gown, to make sure it is ready by noon tomorrow."

"That'll cost Mr. Penkridge a pound or two."

"I suppose he figures it's small enough investment, if his daughter can snare the likes of Lord Whitfield."

"And what, may I ask, do you plan to wear?"

"I haven't given it much thought."

"Then stop and give it some!" Maude said rather sharply, and she saw the blush rise in her niece's cheeks. "I don't mean to be harsh with you, Lila, but you must take more pride in your looks. Why, if you put your mind to it, you could be the loveliest girl in the room tomorrow."

Lila erupted with laughter. "I don't think I'd hold a candle to Jacinda. She's a beauty. I wonder what she'll wear? She's been very closedmouthed about her out fit."

"She probably wants to keep it a secret until the day of the tea, or Hortense is likely to have her seamstress make the identical style and color. I don't think Hortense or that Penkridge woman will ever acquire a flair for taste." Maude set down the tray and moved over to pick up the sugar dish. "You didn't sell your mother's silverware, did you? We'll need the sugar tongs, lemon tongs, and spoons."

"No, I took it out on several occasions, but when the time arrived, I simply couldn't part with it." Lila rubbed another spot on the tray she was cleaning and held it up to the light to inspect it. "Now, thank goodness, maybe I won't have to take it to Mr. Matlock. The Penkridge girls and Jacinda's tuition covers our household expenses with a little to tuck away. As much as I dislike Lord Whitfield, his coming to tea is probably the best thing that could happen for me."

"What do you suppose made him accept a school girl's invitation?" Maude went to the china cabinet to remove the tea cups and dessert plates. "We'll need to wash these since they haven't been used recently. I tell you, this is enough to thrill my old bones. It's the first exciting thing that's happened around here in months." Turning back to Lila, she added, "And you simply must get out a pretty gown for the occasion. I won't have you looking dowdy and frumpy."

"Well, if you keep insisting, I'll own up. I did buy some lace and ribbon this afternoon. I thought you might be able to spruce up one of my old gowns."

"Wonderful! Put down that silver and run upstairs

and fetch it immediately. Let me see what has to be done. And pick a bright, cheerful color. Your mourning period is over and there's no reason to keep wearing those dark colors." Maude put down her polishing rag. "I'll be in the parlor. Let me get my mending basket and see what we can do to that gown." She started off, not wanting to waste another minute.

Lila did as told without even a hint of protest. She ran to retrieve her gown, because secretly, although she didn't want Maude to know it, she was anxious to look her best tomorrow afternoon. She attributed this anxiety to feminine pride, but she also wanted to impress Lord Whitfield for some inexplicable reason. Jacinda and the Penkridge sisters were bound to outdress her, since their gowns would be new; still she wanted to look as pretty as possible.

Lila had already selected the gown she liked best. It was a bright jonquil of thin muslim over a slip of darker yellow, high waisted, with a low round neckline and tiny puffed sleeves. Just before her father's accident, he had won a hundred pounds during one of his lucky nights at the faro tables and had come home in a jovial mood. He had slipped a nice sum in her hand and instructed her to go to the seamstress and have several new frocks stitched. The jonquil had been her favorite because it made her feel bright, lightheaded and so wonderfully frivolous. Sadly she paused for a moment and tried to think of the last time she had felt as happy as when the jonquil gown was bought.

Lila shook off the sudden feeling of self pity, and grabbed up the gown from the bed where she had lain it. She scooped up the small package of lace and ribbon and took it with her, growing excited at the prospect of having a pretty new frock.

"Here it is, what do you think?" Lila asked breathlessly as she entered the parlor and held the dress in front of her for Maude's scrutiny. "And please don't say you don't like it, because it's the best I have to offer."

Maude studied the fabric and turned the gown over and over for a few minutes. "I like the color, and although the style had changed a little, the material is of good quality and that doesn't go out of vogue. Let me see what you bought to adorn it. It's a tad too plain."

Excited over her aunt's initial approval, Lila quickly dumped the ribbon and lace on the table. "I thought you might put a little trim on it or something."

"Yes, yes. I like this. I'll add the ribbon around the sleeves and pull up the shirt a bit and tack it in place. I have a large rose made of silk which will fit perfectly there. In last month's issue of the *Ladies Monthly Museum* there was a fashion plate showing the exact same style." Maude chuckled. "If you don't take care, you'll outshine your charges and steal both their prospective suitors."

Lila giggled at such a thought, and twirled once more around the room. "Lord Haydon seems a decent sort, but they are welcome to Lord Whitfield." She said this, but secretly it was Whitfield she most wanted to surprise with her improved appearance.

"Do you have any slippers to match this gown?"

"I have a pair of white kidskin which will have to do. There was never enough money to get shoes dyed to match all my gowns, like other girls have." She glanced at her aunt knowingly. "You know how Papa was. A hundred pounds won tonight, two hundred pounds spent tomorrow at the tailors or gaming houses, so I settled for practical basic colors."

"You always were a levelheaded girl." Maude stood and started toward the sitting room for her needle and thread. "Can you finish the polishing and cleaning in the dining room so I can get to work on this? Nettie and Rose will have so much to do in the morning that the silver and china need to be readied tonight. We simply must have it lovely by tomorrow."

THE FOLLOWING MORNING the household was up early and all abuzz with excitement before the girls even arrived for classes. Every room shone, draperies had been dusted, pillows plumped up, and china and silver sparkled on the tea tray, which sat on the dining table, waiting to be filled.

When ten o'clock came and the girls finally arrived, it was all Lila could do to keep their minds on the lessons as they constantly checked the clock. Finally at noon, Lila closed her French book and told the girls to eat their lunch quickly, so they could go upstairs and dress.

Mrs. Penkridge sent her maid around at half past the hour to help her daughters get dressed, while Rose was instructed to help Jacinda and then come to Lila's room to help her.

The house was aflutter with excitement, giggling, screeches of hysteria and much prancing about before the mirrors; however, fifteen minutes before the appointed two o'clock, all the girls were back in the parlor, looking their best.

Lila, dressed in her yellow gown, moved carefully through the group examining their attire.

"Hortense, that's such a lovely shade on you. Is it a blue?" Lila inspected the girl's hair and nodded her approval. The soft Grecian curls added a softness to the Penkridge sharp nose and the hint of rouge heightened her pale English cheeks.

"The color is called bishop's blue, Miss Appleby." Hortense curtsied and whipped out her ivory fan and began fanning furiously.

"Not too vigorously, Hortense. We don't want to blow the gentlemen away. Fan like this." Lila snapped open her white feather fan and brushed it back and forth coquettishly.

Jacinda and Idelia popped open their fans and began practicing too, between peals of giggles.

"Young ladies, stop that infernal giggling," reprimanded Maude. "We don't want our gentlemen callers to think this is the school for hoydens, now do we?" Maude had put on her fine black silk gown with ruffles down the front. It was not at all in the latest fashion, but older women did not have to compete for a suitor's attentions. She wore with it a double strand of perfectly matched pearls that cascaded nearly to her waist. That and the sunburst diamond pin were two of her most prized pieces of jewelry from her late husband. And surprisingly they turned her from a plain matron into a lady of genteel means.

Lila passed on down the line of girls, inspecting Idelia with a critical eye. The girl stood nervously and fidgeted in her dress of pink muslin which was very becoming on her small frame. She had pulled her blond hair back and tied it with a large velvet bow which matched her gown and shoes. Lila nodded her approval. "You look absolutely charming, my dear. Now go and sit by the fireplace in your designated spot."

"Yes, ma'am," said Idelia. "I hope I won't have to speak, though, ma'am. I'd really rather not."

"Nonsense, child. Of course you'll enter into the conversation. Why wouldn't you?"

"It's my teeth. They aren't straight, and I don't want the gentlemen to notice."

Lila laughed and clucked, snapping her fan shut and tapping the girl on the shoulder lightly. "Idelia, you are a sweet-natured young lady with a pleasant personality. A pretty smile will wipe all thoughts of your teeth out of a swain's mind. Now, go and do as I say. If you make a gentleman feel at ease and charm him with a sweet story, a crooked tooth won't matter a whit to him. Now scoot!"

The girl's face glowed and she smiled shyly. "I'm so excited. This is the first time I've ever taken company. What a thrill, and two earls to boot!"

"Hush now and get to your seat." Lila moved on to Jacinda, who stood confidently, waiting to hear her compliments. "Jacinda, in that bottle green gown and square neckline you look absolutely divine. Is that a new Paris fashion?"

"Yes, ma'am. Mother had it made for me on her last trip to France."

"Well, I approve one hundred percent." Lila glanced

around the room at her charges and smiled with satisfaction. "I must say, you are wonderful charges. You look like . . . like . . ."

"A bouquet of flowers," said Jacinda, which sent them all into peals of laughter again.

"Miss Appleby, even you look different this afternoon," said Hortense gazing at her. "I'd never noticed how beautiful you are until you put on that yellow gown. In the past you've always worn those dull old browns."

"Thank you, Hortense, for the compliment. However, you must not tell your elders of things you don't like about them."

Hortense blushed. "I didn't mean to be critical."

"No, dear, I understand." Lila glanced around the room, inspecting the last final details. Everything appeared to be ready. Roses had been cut early that morning while the dew was still on them, so they would remain lovely all day. They now stood on the end table and in the foyer, and a massive arrangement of multicolored ones in a silver wine cooler adorned the mantle. Their fragrance drifted sweetly through the air. Aunt Maude's crocheted doilies rested on the back of the sofa and on the arms of the chairs. Lila smiled with satisfaction at how the small crocheted pieces gave new life to the the worn furniture's appearance.

Jacinda said, "Miss Appleby, you must wear bright colors more often. You look sparkling in that yellow." Idelia nodded her agreement.

Maude smiled at her niece. "That's exactly what I've been trying to tell her for weeks, and now perhaps she'll listen. Lila, you do look different this afternoon.

Did you add a touch of rouge or are you a bit excited like the rest of us?"

Lila glanced in the large gilt-edged mirror that hung on the wall near the piano, and saw her reflection with the colorful roses in the background. Even she was stunned at what a cozy scene it made. Unconsciously she fingered the heirloom diamond broach that she wore pinned to the corner of the square neckline on her gown. The muslin had turned modish under Maude's deft skill with her needle.

Jacinda stood and walked gracefully over to the window and peeped out. "I think I see Lord Haydon and Lord Whitfield leaving Brighton Hall. Oh, it is them!"

"Jacinda, come away from the window quickly. We mustn't let them see us watching for their arrival. Now girls, let's wait patiently for our guests. Hortense, would you like to pour the tea?"

"Oh, Miss Appleby, must I?" All the color drained from her cheeks and she fanned herself nervously.

"I'll do it," offered Idelia.

Hortense and Jacinda groaned, shaking their heads vigorously. "No, you might spill the pot on poor Lord Whitfield's leg and scald him. Imagine a rake as handsome as he, scarred for life by a clumsy chit with a hot pot of tea," said Hortense, putting her hand to her forehead melodramatically. They doubled over with a fit of the giggles.

"Why don't we set rules as to who must pour? If Lord Haydon sits nearest the tea tray, then I'll volunteer to pour. I do think he's the most divine—"

"Jacinda, that's no way for a lady to behave. Now

you're all here to learn the social graces. Hortense is the oldest, so she will be first."

"Oh, no, does that mean the gentlemen will think I'm on the shelf?" Hortense shook her curls vigorously. "I don't think I can do it."

Lila went to the girl, patting her comfortingly on the shoulder. "Now listen, Hortense, you're a very adept young lady. All you need is practice. We've done this a dozen times in rehearsal. I'm certain you'll do a splendid job or I wouldn't assign you this duty. Now, sit up straight and show us all what a wonderful hostess you are."

"I can do it, can't I?" Hortense brightened, her confidence restored under Lila's praise.

There was a firm knock on the front door and at that moment all conversation ended. The girls listened for Nettie's footsteps in the front hall. Even Lila found her heart skipping a beat, which annoyed her immensely because it was beginning to happen every time Lord Whitfield drew near.

"Come in, milords, the ladies be expecting you in the parlor." Nettie led the way into the silent room, and Lila moved gracefully toward the door.

"So glad to see you, Lord Haydon and Lord Whitfield." She held out her hand and Lord Whitfield took it in his own, bowing low. His lips brushed a light kiss on it.

"Miss Appleby, you must wear that shade of yellow more often. I'm astounded at the change it makes in your appearance. I'd hardly recognize you as the same person. Isn't that true, Haydon?"

"Miss Appleby has always been an enchanting

neighbor, Whitfield. You must have recognized that already." Lord Haydon bent over and kissed Lila's hand, too.

While Lila appreciated Haydon's praise, it was Whitfield's touch that flustered her for a moment, but she quickly regained her composure and turned to the girls. "Please be seated and I'll ring for tea."

"I'll sit by the lovely Miss Kingsbury, if I may," said Lord Haydon, moving to the settee where Jacinda sat coyly fanning, gazing up at him through large green eyes.

For a moment Hortense frowned, but Lord Whitfield moved swiftly to her side and took his place. She immediately shot a smug look toward Jacinda, but the gesture was lost on the girl, because she and Haydon were already engaged in lively conversation.

Nettie returned with the tea and Hortense began the task of serving it while Lila sat beside Aunt Maude and Idelia, nervously watching every move to make certain Hortense made no mistakes. To her credit Hortense performed the task beautifully, and Lila was only sorry Mrs. Penkridge couldn't be present to witness the miracle she had performed in the once clumsy girl.

After everyone had been served, Lila was able to sit back and enjoy the lively chatter and study the gentlemen more closely. Haydon was dashing in his yellow double-breasted tailcoat and sand-colored trousers with midcalf Hessian boots, but it was Lord Whitfield who cut the sharpest figure.

Through slightly lowered eyelashes, she sipped her tea and studied him over the brim of her cup. He sat comfortably, his legs crossed, accenting his handsome calves in the tight doeskin trousers and blue velvet tail-coat with its white lace stock reaching to the edge of his black hair. Lila had to concede he was a handsome devil. When he leaned closer to catch the words Hortense uttered, it was easy to understand how he charmed the ladies of London. Even she had to keep reminding herself that he was far too worldly for her and completely out of her reach.

When tea was finished and the cups collected, Lord Whitfield turned to Lila and said, "Would you ladies honor us with some of the songs you've been practicing? I often hear your lively music as I'm about my grounds."

Lila blushed when she remembered how terrible some of their playing had been.

"Let Miss Appleby sing," cried Idelia. "She has the sweetest voice. And who should we get to play for her?"

"Why don't we ask Hortense?" suggested Lila, trying to pick her best student.

"Oh, no, I'd rather sit here and entertain Lord Whitfield. Idelia, you're the best pianist. You accompany Miss Appleby."

"That's a splendid idea!" added Jacinda, glancing seductively at Haydon, whom she had practically groveling by this time.

Rather flustered by the idea, Lila nonetheless went to stand by the piano. She knew it would not be polite to force the group to beg her.

She and Idelia decided on the pieces they were to perform and the music program began. Lila had sung only a few verses when she caught Lord Whitfield staring at her with an odd expression on his face. It actually appeared to be fascination, and she almost skipped a note or two, his rapt attention startled her so.

When they had completed four songs to a hearty round of applause, Lila announced that the concert was over. To her surprise it had been a very enjoyable afternoon and she had forgotten her troubles for the first time in months.

Before Lila realized it, it was time for the gentlemen to depart, as it was not proper for them to visit more than a brief time.

At the door, Lord Whitfield took her hand and said, "My dear Miss Appleby, this has been one of the most pleasant afternoons I've spent since my return to London. I wish to thank you for inviting us. I also would enjoy continuing our newfound friendship and would like to escort you and your aunt to Covent Garden for its next performance Friday evening a week, if you would so honor me."

Lila had to struggle to prevent her mouth falling open in utter disbelief. She had thought he was interested in Hortense. Out of the corner of her eye she had watched with envy as he sat listening to Hortense's every word as though it were profound. And what would Hortense and her mother say should Lila accept the invitation? She glanced around, but the others were out of hearing. Even Aunt Maude was too far away to rescue her. A slight blush rose to her cheeks as she hesitated, wanting so to go, yet afraid.

"Well, my lovely neighbor, what is your answer?" Lord Whitfield looked down at her, a twinkle in his eye.

"I . . . I'd like that very much," Lila stammered, still too surprised to know what else to say. It annoyed her that she stood like a tongue-tied chit in Lord Whitfield's presence. Before she could think of more to say, the others joined them in the foyer and farewells were exchanged.

Once their guests were departed, Lila and the girls moved back into the parlor and collapsed into their chairs, anxious to discuss all that had taken place. It had been a splendid tea.

Lila scarcely heard the girls' lively chatter as she continued to think of her upcoming trip to the opera. Oh, how she had longed to see the new opera house, and until now the ticket had been beyond her budget. She tried to tell herself that was her only reason for accepting, but in truth, her heart fluttered at the thought of being in Lord Whitfield's company again.

Chapter 7

LILA THOUGHT A great deal about Lord Whitfield and his friend Lord Haydon in the days that followed. She began to relent in her harsh opinion of Whitfield until the afternoon Jacinda disappeared.

Lila and her aunt were sitting in the parlor taking a short break when the girls approached Lila and asked to go out in the yard for a nature walk.

It had rained all morning, but around noon the sun swept from behind clouds and the day grew radiant. Lila raised the windows to let the warm spring breeze drift through the room.

"Miss Appleby, may we go outside and study the new flowers? We want to see who can name the most varieties," Jacinda asked innocently.

Lila hesitated for a moment, although she saw no harm in such a venture. Horticulture was a wonderful part of their educations, and every English woman tended a flower garden. She saw the wisdom in the girls learning the various varieties of tulips, roses, and flowering shrubs as well as the other garden plants.

Still, something warned Lila that Jacinda's interest in learning was suddenly more intense than it had been at any point since her schooling began. It was possible, however, that Lord Haydon's fascination with Jacinda had helped her realize the importance of learning skills she'd been reluctant to consider in the past.

Seeing Lila's hesitation, Idelia took her hand and said, "Please, Miss Appleby. Look what a beautiful day it's turned out to be. It would be shame for us to stay cooped up in here with this boring musical piece, when we could be learning all about nature. Don't you agree?" The girl gave Lila her most pleading gaze.

Laughing, Lila relented and said, "You girls know exactly how to worm your way around my instructions, but I must agree it's a lovely day. All right, run along. Now be sure to stay in the back garden. There are plenty of species of tubular plants beginning to bloom in the formal garden by the small fish pond."

A cheer went up and the girls dashed to put on pelisses and bonnets before Lila could add more stipulations.

"I'll be out in a little while to see who can name the most varieties," Lila called after their disappearing backs.

"They are really sweet girls once you get to know them, aren't they?" asked Maude, picking up her sewing and beginning to stitch. "I'm growing very fond of them. Lila, your once gawky ducklings are turning into swans before our very eyes." She rummaged through her yarn basket searching for the exact shade of thread she needed to embroider a purple lily on a new doily. "Have you decided what you plan to wear to the opera Friday night? I hate to keep bringing it up, but if you have sewing for me, I need to get started on it."

"I found a light blue gown which I think will do. If I attach a new bouquet of flowers and nip it in at the waist, as I seem to have lost a few pounds since Father's death, it should do fine." Lila crossed to the window where she watched the girls moving from flower bed to flower bed, occasionally picking up an especially large or colorful variety. "They look so innocent out there, having fun and sharing secrets. Sometimes I forget why their mothers sent them to me."

"They're fine young ladies, and you've done wonders for them already." Maude snipped a thread and laid down her needlework. "Now run upstairs and get that gown."

Lila felt lighthearted and almost girlish herself this afternoon, so she obeyed her aunt without an argument. When she reached her room she slipped into the gown and went quickly downstairs for it to be fitted and altered.

Turning slowly for her aunt to nip a place here and make a tuck there, she said, "You must hurry. I can't leave the girls out there alone for too long or their mothers might not think I'm earning my money."

"Shush! Just let a one of them tell me that."

"Well, what matters is that they continue paying me. Those pounds are keeping us afloat at last, and I don't want to do anything to jeopardize this arrangement."

"I do think it was a clever idea of yours to invite Lord Whitfield and his friend for tea."

"To be honest it was Jacinda who did it, and at the time I was appalled at her forwardness, but I must concede that all turned out well. In fact, Lord Haydon appeared absolutely enamored of our Jacinda."

"I can understand why. She's a lovely young girl."

"And Lord Whitfield paid wonderful attention to Hortense. It was exactly the kind of experience she needs to gain more self-confidence."

"And you didn't do so badly yourself. Lord Whitfield squiring us to the opera gives me hope for your future, too."

"Oh, no, that's ridiculous. I think he merely invited me to repay us for the tea invitation."

"Don't you think for a minute that he did it merely to be polite. I saw the way he kept watching you."

"Aunt Maude, he did no such thing. He spent almost the entire afternoon chatting with Hortense. It was only to be polite that he included me in the conversation from time to time."

"Well, think what you like, but I saw the way he gazed at you while you sang. The man was intrigued."

"Probably couldn't believe how horrible my voice is." Lila whirled and swished her skirt around. "That feels fine. Now let me run and change, so I can go out in the garden before the girls think I've deserted them."

Within a few minutes Lila had redressed and rushed out the back door. She began searching for the girls, but they were nowhere in sight. "Now where can they have gone?" she muttered to herself. "I told them not to leave the yard."

The Appleby yard was large, but since money had grown tight, the hedges had not been trimmed as often as needed, so some had grown over ten feet tall during the winter. Standing down in the maze it was impossible to see the far end of the garden. Lila moved quickly in the direction where she had last seen the girls from the parlor window. Stopping, she listened, but no sounds of their chatter reached her ears, nor did she hear footsteps in the soft, thick carpet of grass.

Everything smelled clean and fresh after the morning rain and the birds chirped happily. A robin flew by and lit in the water fountain for a drink.

"Where are those girls?" Lila said, beginning to grow irritated with them. She had specifically instructed them not to leave the Appleby premises.

"Hortense! Idelia! Jacinda! Where are you?" She came to the end of her property and still there was no sight of the girls.

Lila moved quickly to the back gate, but she saw that it was locked, so they could not have left by it. Turning she made her way around the maze and into the side yard nearest Lord Whitfield's house.

She had walked only a few hundred feet when she at last caught a glimpse of Hortense's plum-colored gown, and she moved rapidly toward the little group.

Hortense and Idelia were sitting on a marble bench sorting their flowers and giggling mischievously. Lila smiled as she approached and took a seat on the bench across from them. "My! That was a brisk little walk. I didn't know what had happened to you." Catching her breath, she glanced around. "Where's Jacinda?"

Idelia glanced over at her sister and giggled, but remained silent. Hortense continued sorting flowers as though she had not heard Lila. Sensing something was amiss, Lila stood and move over to the girls, unconsciously placing her hands on her hips and planting her feet firmly. "Girls, where is Jacinda?"

Hortense shrugged and glanced up from her pile of flowers for the first time. "Isn't she out gathering more tulips?"

"No, she is not. I can see the tulip beds from here, and Jacinda is nowhere to be seen." Lila studied the girls more closely. "You both know where she is, so own up." Seeing their resistance, she changed her tone, speaking more sternly in her best teacher voice. "I demand to know this minute, or I shall have to tell your mother you have been disrespectful."

Hortense remained stubbornly silent. Lila whirled and turned on Idelia. "Young lady, you tell me this instant! She hasn't gone out unchaperoned has she?"

"Oh, no, ma'am. She just went through the garden gate."

"The garden gate?" Lila was mystified for a moment. "How can that be? The gate is locked and the key is in the pantry." She studied the girls, who giggled and gave each other knowing glances.

Then it dawned on Lila. There was a gate between her house and Lord Whitfield's. "She hasn't gone over to Lord Whitfield's has she?" The disbelief and fear rose in Lila by the second. Jacinda was a wild one, and she had known it from the start. Was she over in Lord

Whitfield's house losing her virtue at this moment? Or her reputation at the least? Lila would be ruined if such a thing happened. They could come haul her away to debtor's prison, because her school would be shunned if one of her students fell into disgrace. Silently she groaned.

Turning, she instructed the girls, "Go in to Aunt Maude immediately and begin arranging your flowers. You may each take home a bouquet as a gift for your mother. Don't you think that will be a wonderful surprise for her?" Lila knew the girls were not the least deceived by her calm manner. She wanted them out of hearing in case there was a scandal. How had she allowed herself be duped by the young chit?

She herded the girls to the front door and called to Aunt Maude, who came to see what the problem was.

"Did you have a lovely walk?" asked Maude, not aware that anything was wrong until she caught sight of Lila's face.

"I must run next door and find Jacinda. She wandered over to pick flowers and probably doesn't realize the time is drawing near for her carriage to arrive."

"She isn't picking flowers," said Idelia, quickly. "She's meeting Lord Haydon for an assignation—is that the word, Hortense?"

"Never mind," snapped Lila. "Now go with Aunt Maude and find some pretty vases for your flowers."

Looking nervously at Maude, Lila signaled her to remain calm. "I'll be back in a moment."

"Will Jacinda be sent home in disgrace?" asked Idelia innocently. "She told us about being expelled from her last school."

"We'll discuss this after I've brought her home. Now, should your carriage arrive before I return, I trust that you will keep this confidential until I've had a chance to discuss it with Jacinda."

"Oh, we wouldn't dare tell Mama or she'd remove us from your school in the morning, and we like it here, Miss Appleby," said Idelia again.

Lila shot a silent plea to her aunt before turning to leave. She rushed down the steps and around the side of her house, heading for the gate at close to a run. She had to find Jacinda before her carriage arrived, or she knew her school was doomed. And it was Lord Whitfield she found herself most angry with. He had no business associating with men who were not gentlemen. How dare he allow such a thing to go on under his very roof? Once this was settled, she intended to march over and give him what for.

Lila rushed through the gate and into Lord Whitfield's side yard. His estate, being much larger than her own, contained several acres and Lila paused to look around. Where would she go, if she were meeting a lover? Almost instantly she spied the green top of the gazebo, which she remembered having seen from her second-story window, and headed for it.

When she was within a few yards of it, she heard the tinkle of Jacinda's laughter and gave a sigh of relief. At least the little baggage was not in Lord Whitfield's bedchambers.

Lila called out to the couple as she rounded the corner. There was no need slipping up on them if they were in a compromising position. The gentleman, who had his back to Lila, sprang away from Jacinda and dropped his hands to his sides. It was evident the young lovers had been in a very passionate embrace.

"Miss Appleby!" Jacinda sprang to her feet, straightening her gown and grabbing up her bouquet of wilting flowers.

"Jacinda," said Lila, trying to control her anger and not snatch the girl away from Lord Haydon and drag her home. "I think we need to be on our way, don't you?" The words sounded soft and sweet, but anger lay just below the surface.

"I came over to see some lovely roses Lord Haydon told me were blooming in the rose garden. I must have let the time slip away." Jacinda said this as glibly as a school girl accustomed to pleasing her teacher with little surprises.

What a professional liar she is, thought Lila, impressed despite herself with the girl's blasé behavior. Most girls would have burst into tears and begun pleading not to be exposed to their mothers.

"Miss Appleby, I can assure you nothing improper took place. Miss Kingsbury is a dear young lady, and if anyone is to blame, it is I."

"You are absolutely correct about that Lord Haydon, and I shall speak with you later about this matter. While Jacinda used poor judgment in coming over here, you showed less than gentlemanly behavior in encouraging her. She is no more than a child. You sir, are supposed to be a gentleman."

Lila snatched the speechless Jacinda by the hand and marched off, leaving Lord Haydon standing speechless. But Lila caught the smug glance Jacinda cast in his direction and even his return wink was not missed by her.

Once they were back on the Appleby property, Jacinda tried to pull away from Lila's grasp and said, "Are you going to tell my mother?"

"Should I?" asked Lila, staring closely at the girl. She really didn't think anything more than a quick kiss had happened, however, she had to prevent a second meeting.

"Nothing happened, Miss Appleby. I promise."

"Don't you realize how fragile a young lady's reputation is?"

Jacinda shrugged. "Oh, that's all right. Mine already is ruined according to my mother. There's no harm to be had from this afternoon."

"No harm? Young lady, don't you realize Idelia and Hortense could be hurt by your behavior, too?" Lila gestured around her helplessly. "Why, if this should get out, my school will be ruined."

Jacinda took her hand. "Oh, Miss Appleby. I don't want that to happen. I like you and your school. Please, don't tell my mother, and I promise it will never happen again."

Lila felt her anger melting. She did like the girl. Jacinda was sweet, witty, and too pretty for her own good. Lila did not want to disrupt the class, so she relented. "All right. This time I shall remain silent, but if it ever happens again, I simply can't take the responsibility."

"Thank you," cried Jacinda, leaning over and hugging Lila impulsively. "I promise to be more careful in the future."

Lila shook her head. "Not more careful, my dear, but less like the great unwashed and more like the genteel lady you are born to be."

"But Miss Appleby, you don't understand. It's been so long since you were a young girl that you've forgotten all about the wonderful rapture of being in love." As if this excused everything, Jacinda flashed her most glowing smile and said, "I'm in love. I'm in love with Lord Haydon and he with me!"

"This is certainly more than I'm skilled at handling. I suggest you tell your Lord Haydon to pay a call at your home and talk to your father. After he gets proper permission to come calling on you, then what you and he do will be your affair. But until then, I absolutely refuse to take the responsibility for watching you every minute. Do you understand this, young lady?"

Seeing that this lecture was having little or no effect on her charge, Lila switched tactics. She smiled and confessed, "I have been in love once or twice myself, so I do understand the things you're feeling. But you must go about this courtship in the proper way. No more slipping off to meet him unchaperoned. Is that clear?"

The sound of carriages pulling up out front interrupted them. "I'll run get my reticule. I think that's my carriage." Anxious to be gone, Jacinda raced off.

"Jacinda, you walk like a lady. No more running," Lila called after her, letting out a deep sigh and shaking her head. The girl was so bubbly that it was impossible to stay angry with her more than a few minutes.

"Yes, Miss Appleby," Jacinda shouted over her shoulder, slowing her pace considerably.

* * *

"IT SIMPLY CAN'T be helped, Aunt Maude. I've got to go over and talk to Lord Whitfield about Jacinda and Lord Haydon. He can't allow such carryings-on in his own yard." Lila moved toward the door without the usual lightness in her step. She dreaded having to reproach Lord Whitfield, but there wasn't a man of the house to send over, so she was elected for the job.

"He was such a gentleman the other day. Lila, why must you stir up things?"

"We thought Lord Haydon was a gentleman, too, didn't we? And look what he did. Schemed to rendez-vous with Jacinda." She shook her head. "No, Aunt Maude, my school is more important than Lord Whit-field's friendship, and I don't expect him to get upset. I believe he'll be on my side this time." Lila reached the door and turned back to add one last word. "I will be back within the hour. It shouldn't take long to get this matter settled."

"I'm working on your gown for the opera. I do hope you don't go over there and do something to ruin your chances with Lord Whitfield."

Lila laughed. "I have no chances with the man. Re-sign yourself to the fact that I'll spend the rest of my life teaching awkward girls to be ladies, dear aunt. As I've told you before, the invitation was extended merely to repay our hospitality. Nothing more." With those words, Lila sailed out the door and down the front steps. Secretly she was afraid of exactly what her aunt feared, that her very fragile relationship with the handsome rake was about to end. And the thought made her very sad, because he did have a very charming and disarming personality.

Lila lifted her chin high and marched up to the front door of Brighton Hall. She gave the brass knocker a resounding thump and stood nervously waiting to be admitted.

This time the butler recognized her and opened the door warmly. "Come in Miss Appleby. His lordship is in the library. Please wait here and I shall announce you."

"Is Lord Haydon still here, too? I wish to speak with him also, if he is."

"No ma'am. I believe he left quite hurriedly a short while ago."

"I should think he did," Lila mumbled under her breath as the butler moved down the corridor.

She studied the hall while she waited. On her last visit she had been so nervous that she had not really noticed the decorations. The hall was large, with a marble floor that sparkled from a recent cleaning. The usual line of family portraits stared back at her through cold, unfriendly eyes. There was only one picture that intrigued her, and it was of a woman, dressed in a white gown, wearing a large diamond necklace and holding a rose. Lord Whitfield's mother, perhaps? She couldn't decide.

"Excuse me, Miss, Lord Whitfield will see you now."

Lila nearly jumped, she had been so engrossed in the portrait that she had failed to hear the butler's return.

Walking briskly down the corridor, she followed the butler to her destination.

As she entered the large library, Lord Whitfield was

signing his name with a flourish on a document. Seeing her, he quickly sanded and blotted the ink and stood to greet her.

"Come in, Miss Appleby. What brings you over to see me so soon? It's a delightful surprise." He came around his desk and took her hand, kissing it elegantly. "Here, let's move to the chairs near the fire. The afternoon has turned rather chilly."

"Lord Whitfield, I can't stay long. I have a most unpleasant situation to discuss with you."

His eyebrows rose in surprise. "It can't be my behavior again, Miss Whitfield. What can I have done to cause such a frown to cross your very attractive face?"

"Your friend Lord Haydon coaxed Miss Kingsbury into meeting him in your gazebo out back for, I fear, less than honorable purposes."

"Is that what she told you?"

"Well, no, but I saw them together with my own eyes." Lila felt the heat rise in her cheeks. Was he going to make light of the matter? She was stunned.

"Lord Haydon explained his side of the story, and I don't think he planned the event." He glared at her. "You must admit Miss Kingsbury is a lovely lady, and if she wished his company, he most certainly didn't intend to avoid her."

"I didn't want to have to mention this, but I caught them in an embrace."

"Is there something wrong with that?"

"Lord Whitfield! He was kissing her!"

"It seems a natural enough thing to do to me." He shrugged and grinned rakishly. "I can't say that I don't envy him the opportunity."

"You can't be serious." Lila gasped in shock and stared at him, her anger rising by the moment. She had not expected this, although now she realized this was the typical reaction of a blade like Whitfield.

"They are smitten with each other. Lord Haydon is absolutely besotted by her."

"That does not give him the right to kiss her," Lila argued heatedly.

"Have you never been in love, Miss Appleby?" He moved closer and studied her face closely, observing the slow color rising in her cheeks. He chuckled. "I don't believe you have."

Whitfield circled Lila staring at her intently, a roguish grin spread across his lips. "You haven't been in love, have you, Miss Appleby? You really have never experienced the joy of an affair of the heart."

"Really, sir, your attitude is repulsive to me. I find it most annoying that you should pry into my personal affairs. You really don't know a thing about me." Her chin jutted out stubbornly as she tried to match his stare. But his eyes held a twinkle that absolutely made her heart flutter. "I'm here to discuss my charge, Miss Kingsbury. Her rendezvous with Lord Haydon must not be repeated."

"Shouldn't Haydon be the one you take this matter up with? It seems none of my affair."

Lila inhaled deeply and nodded. "You're correct, my lord, but he isn't here, is he? And the ugly business took place on your property." She tried to appeal to his gentlemanly nature, although she was about to decide he didn't have an honorable bone in his body. "I thought you might have a word with Lord Haydon and ask him not . . . not to encourage the girl. She's really quite young and at a most impressionable age."

"Humph! I'd say she's far more worldly than you, my dear." He moved even closer.

"Why must you continue to bring me into this conversation? I find it most disturbing." She really was growing annoyed with him. All he seemed to care about was taunting her.

"I find you most interesting. There are few women today of your age who are quite so naive." He waved his hands and shrugged his shoulders. "An innocent kiss between two lovers, and you are ready to send the poor girl off to a convent and have the gentleman hanged in Newgate Prison."

"I find it most improper for a lady to be meeting a gentleman, especially one of Lord Haydon's reputation, unchaperoned and when she is in my care." She stamped her foot. "No, it simply must not happen again or I shall be forced to tell Jacinda's mother. Even if it means the end to my school." She appealed to him again. "Can't you understand how important this matter is?"

"And I continue to argue that you are placing too much importance on an innocent kiss," he argued stubbornly.

"I disagree, my lord. How can you call a kiss innocent?"

"I don't believe you've ever been kissed." A grin crossed his lips. "That's it, isn't it? You've never experienced one, therefore you think it's the spawn of the devil."

He moved dangerously near and Lila backed against

the edge of his desk, trying to flee. He stood so close now that she felt his warmth and smelled his spicy cologne. Her heart pounded so loudly that it was impossible for her to breathe or think clearly.

"I was brought up to believe a lady was betrothed before she allowed herself to be kissed," she argued stubbornly as he moved even closer. Her voice, scarce louder than a whisper, betrayed her nervousness.

"Such old-fashioned beliefs. There's rarely a chit past sixteen who hasn't stolen an innocent kiss at one time or another," he said, shaking his head, the twinkle in his eye making him even more rakish and handsome. "I think it's time we enriched your education, Miss Appleby."

"My lord, you can't mean to do what I think?" Lila stared up into his eyes and placing her hand over her heart, trying to slow its crazy fluttering, for his look warned her that she was about to receive her first kiss.

"Only to prove my point," he said huskily as he put his hands on her slender shoulders and drew her to him.

Lila uttered a slight gasp, her mouth forming a perfect little pucker just as his lips touched hers. The warm sensation sent a charge through her body and she felt limp and unable to resist another second.

She knew it was wrong, but the feel of his warm lips on hers tingled so wonderfully that for a few moments the world didn't exist and she succumbed to the pleasure. No wonder people were always wanting to do this, she reasoned, it felt wonderful.

Suddenly, Lord Whitfield, who seemed to be enjoying this far more than he'd expected, drew her closer, his lips burning into hers. Finally, she came to her senses and her eyes flew open. Pushing with all her might, she shoved him away, and gasped for breath. "Lord Whitfield, how dare you?"

He stepped back and bowed gracefully, a broad smile crossing his handsome face. "Please accept my apology, but I had to make my point. You see, you are the same. An innocent kiss did not change you in the slightest."

That's all you know, she thought. For Lila realized she had fallen madly in love. Without another word she bolted from his study and out the front door, the echo of his laughter ringing in her ears.

Chapter 8

"YOU AREN'T GOING to the opera? Why not?" asked Maude, thoroughly confused. "I thought you had waited for over a year to see the new Royal Opera House." Sometimes her niece mystified her.

"It's Lord Whitfield. I don't want to be in his presence."

"Now that's the most confusing thing of all. He's a handsome devil with the charm to match." Seeing that this was not the tack to take with Lila, she switched her strategy. "Besides, I want to attend the opera. You can't wish to deny me this opportunity."

Lila took her aunt's shoulders and hugged her affectionately. "I know how much you want to go, but it's simply impossible for me." She didn't want to tell her aunt that she had fallen foolishly, hopelessly in love with the most unsuitable of suitors, and even worse, she had compromised her reputation by enjoying—yes, enjoying—a kiss with him. She still remembered the wonderful tingle of his lips on hers, and also the terrible sound of his laughter as she had bolted from his house, unable to say another word in defense of her argument against Jacinda and Lord Haydon.

"Does Lord Whitfield know that you don't intend to honor his invitation?" Maude studied the girl closely. She hadn't been herself since she came storming back from Whitfield's the previous day. In fact, she had rather expected Lila to chastise Jacinda and the Penkridge girls for their behavior, but instead Lila had held her morning lessons as though nothing had taken place. A wise decision in Maude's opinion, but definitely out of character for Lila. She had always felt the girl a tad too prudish for her own good.

"I feel confident he'll not show his face over here."

Maude threw up her hands and shrugged. "Well, your gown is ready and your bath water has been drawn, so you might as well get dressed."

"I shall bathe and prepare for an early bed. This has been a most tiring day and I'm exhausted." Lila rang for Nettie to come help her undress and bathe.

Shaking her head, Maude left the room. She was already dressed for the opera in her best black silk gown and she didn't intend changing until bedtime. The hall clock struck seven, which meant it was too early to consider bed yet. Disappointment crept into her thoughts, and she felt annoyed with Lila. This was simply too great an opportunity to pass, and she thought Lord Whitfield had shown serious interest in Lila.

Maude had scarcely reached the parlor and picked up her darning needle when she heard a carriage pull up outside and the sound of footsteps approaching. Glancing at the mantle clock she checked the time again, then decided to peep outside and see who could be arriving at this hour unannounced. To her amazement she saw Lord Whitfield alight from his coach. He had come after all! She threw down her darning and rushed to warn Lila. Maude's spirits soared as she dashed toward the stairs, moving as quickly as her old limbs would carry her. There was still hope they might attend the opera after all.

But before Maude put foot to stairstep, Lord Whitfield's knock on the door brought Lila rushing out of her room and down the hallway.

"What is it?" Lila asked glancing from Maude's face to the front door.

"I think it's Lord Whitfield here to take us to the opera," whispered Maude, trying to keep the delight out of her voice. It was all she could do not to add, "I told you so."

"Well, we simply aren't going," said Lila brushing past her aunt and moving swiftly toward the door. She squared her shoulders, lifted her chin high and opened the door, while Maude and Nettie stood silently watching, not sure what was going on, but not wanting to miss a word of it.

"Good evening," Lila said coolly as she stared up into Lord Whitfield's piercing brown eyes.

"Why aren't you ready for the opera?" he asked brusquely as he surveyed her disarray.

"Because I'm not going," said Lila stubbornly.

He swept past her and into the foyer, not waiting to be invited. Once in the room, he whirled and frowned down at her with a glare that would have left brave men trembling. "Not going? What sort of foolishness is this?"

"I simply can't discuss it." Lila crossed her arms and returned his stare.

Whitfield stood silent for a few seconds as if not sure what his next move would be, and then a grin spread rakishly across his lips. "It's the kiss, isn't it?" Sure that he had hit upon it, when he saw her cheeks blaze scarlet, he nodded. "That's exactly it. An innocent kiss and you're so prudish you want to make an issue out of it. I tell you, Miss Appleby, go upstairs and get dressed. We are going to the opera!" He turned to Maude who stood completely lost as to what was taking place. "I see you had the good sense to dress. Please accompany your niece upstairs and get her ready. She is going to the opera! Nobody treats me in this manner." His voice boomed out the orders and Maude jumped. She quickly took Lila by the arm.

"Come along, dear, your gown is laid out." Turning to Lord Whitfield, she struggled not to smile with glee. This was exactly the sort of man Lila needed. One who would not let her dictate her every whim. "Please go into the parlor and make yourself comfortable. We won't be long."

Meekly Lila followed her, unable to think of an appropriate comment. She knew she had pushed him as far as he'd go. At that moment Lord Whitfield looked angry enough to dress her himself if she balked.

Once in her room, Lila whirled on her aunt and said, "Why didn't you do something to help me? The man is a raving reprobate. A bully. Can't you see that? Imagine storming in like that and telling me that I will attend the opera with him. I've never heard of such an unchivalrous act."

Maude shoved Lila over to the tub and rang for Rose to come and help Nettie. "Quickly, get your bath, and don't keep Lord Whitfield waiting. I shan't ask what took place between the two of you yesterday, but I do know that Lord Whitfield is exactly the type of man you need to manage you." Maude giggled impishly. "He did a masterful job of taking control downstairs."

"Aunt Maude! How can you say such a thing? The man is a bully. Why, if Father were alive, he'd order him out of this house on the double."

"I doubt that, love, so bathe quickly—here comes Rose. She'll have your hair arranged in no time."

Within a remarkably short length of time Lila found herself gowned and perfumed, her hair twirled into a most becoming knot and held in place with ivory combs.

Stepping back from the mirror she surveyed her appearance, and the reflection she saw lifted her spirits. The blue gown had turned out rather to her liking, and she did want to see the new Opera House. Perhaps an evening with Lord Whitfield would not be too offensive after all.

She pinned a tiny ruby and diamond pin to the shoulder of her gown while she thought of how dashing Lord Whitfield looked this evening. Secretly she admired the way he had taken control of the situation. Smiling, she decided she liked masterful men.

At last satisfied with her appearance, Lila and Maude moved off down the hall.

They entered the parlor a scant thirty minutes late and Lord Whitfield turned and smiled in greeting. "I must say that I'm escorting the two prettiest ladies in London to the opera this evening. Mrs. Watson, you look charming as does Miss Appleby." Lord Whitfield offered an arm to each lady, and the party moved off.

Chapter 9

LILA TOOK LORD Whitfield's hand and allowed him to help her into the carriage. Secretly she was delighted to be going to the opera, although she stubbornly refused to admit it to him. Imagine storming into her parlor and ordering her to get dressed. Why if the *ton* heard of this, she'd be the talk of the circuit. A tiny smile crept to her lips as she thought of making a stir in those hallowed circles.

She sat next to her aunt and Lord Whitfield faced them, carrying on a light conversation with Maude. If he was aware of her silence, he gave no indication.

Lila watched him with awe. He amused her aunt with light banter, leaned close to catch her every word, and even flirted with the elderly woman outrageously, all the while master of the moment. One thing she had to concede—Lord Whitfield was a charmer of the first order.

Before she realized it they were turning down Bow

Street and their carriage drew up behind a long line of coaches delivering the *ton* to the night's performance. Lanterns adorned the outside of the ornate new opera house, built the previous year by Robert Smirke who had chosen to model it after the Temple of Minerva in Athens.

As their carriage made its slow way to the front door, Lila stared up at the ornamental frieze of literary figures carved above its entrance.

"The building is breathtaking," she murmured, unable to remain silent any longer.

"Now aren't you delighted that you decided to accompany us?" asked Whitfield, nodding his agreement. "It would have been a foolish choice to stay home with a book on such a night as this."

Lila still couldn't bring herself to agree with him, but she did grin slyly. "I did expect a more chivalrous greeting," she argued stubbornly.

"If I had been gentle with you, you'd have that pretty little face behind a book now instead of dressed in your frippery and here with us."

Lila was about to reply when Maude stepped in, "Here, here, that's enough such bickering. We're here because Lord Whitfield was gracious enough to invite us, and we shall have a magnificent time."

The carriage halted and a doorman stepped up and opened it immediately. Maude stood and moved gracefully down the steps before turning back and saying excitedly, "Come along, you two, we are running late. I don't want to miss one minute of this event."

Lila felt the same excitement, and not being one prone to sulking, she grinned at Whitfield. "Shall we call a truce and enjoy the evening? I must admit to a certain thrill at being here." She grinned impishly and allowed the doorman to hand her down from the carriage. "And," she whispered to him so no one else could hear, "the kiss meant absolutely nothing to me. So, you were correct on that count, too. Whatever could have made Jacinda act so foolishly over one is a mystery to me."

"Next time I'll have to do a better job," he whispered in her ear.

"There won't be a next time," she snapped, turning and moving rapidly away. The man was maddening. He enjoyed seeing her uncomfortable.

Whitfield easily followed her and seemed about to reply, but instead took her arm and escorted her to the entrance of the opera house which was ablaze with the brilliance of the thousands of candles flickering on the candelabra overhead. Lila felt the burning warmth of his hand on her arm, and she wanted to snatch it from his grasp, but knew to do so would tell him more than she wished for him to know.

So their party moved briskly into the theater, through the magnificent vestibule and up the staircase, past a statue of Shakespeare carved from yellow marble, and into Whitfield's private box. Lila had attended the opera before the original house burned in 1808, but then she had sat in the main floor and wondered what it would be like to see the show from high above the crowd.

They had no more than sat down when the lights dimmed and the music began. Lord Whitfield rested on his small velvet chair, legs crossed, and watched

Lila, amused to see how much she was enjoying the evening. He decided she was far more lovely than he had first thought, with her fair complexion and the light tint of blush her excitement brought to her cheeks. And although she had appeared sullen at the start of the evening, now every time she looked his way she smiled, a twinkle of happiness in her magnificent blue eyes. It annoyed him that he appeared to be falling under her spell, because he had no intention of settling down. No, after tonight he would simply stay his distance from her. However, for the evening, he intended to enjoy her charm.

Leaning close, he whispered in her ear, "Here, take my glasses; you can make out every detail with them. Are you enjoying yourself?"

Turning she realized her face was only inches from his, and she smelled the wonderful odor of his cologne. "Yes," she whispered softly, unconsciously placing her hand on his arm to accent her reply.

He chuckled and drew away, for he had the undeniable urge to kiss the soft round mouth he had found so enticing the day before. The woman was a bewitching nymph, and he didn't understand how he had missed it from the beginning.

Lila turned back to the stage, but soon used the opera glasses to study the finely dressed men and women in the audience below. Never had she seen so many jeweled and gowned ladies and been allowed to study them at her leisure while being lulled by lovely music. It was mesmerizing.

She was also thankful Maude had made touch-ups on her gown, because it did not look unstylish even in this company. Of course, she wore only her small ruby and diamond pin, while other ladies in the crowd wore huge diamonds, emeralds and pearls, yet she did not feel uncomfortable or out of place. A glance at Aunt Maude made her swell with pride—the matron looked very presentable in her black silk and rope of pearls.

Finally she stole a glance at Lord Whitfield. He wore a black velvet long coat and skin-tight black satin breeches with a starched white shirt and cravat. A large diamond stud held his lace-trimmed cravat in place, and she caught a glimpse of gold cufflinks beneath the velvet sleeve. She surveyed the audience, and he was truly the most dashing gentleman present that evening.

When the lights went up for the intermission, she gasped. "It can't be half over," she cried in disbelief.

"Shall we go down for some refreshments, or would you ladies like to stay here and I'll bring us some punch?" Whitfield stood and waited for them to decide.

Lila sprang to her feet immediately. "Oh, I want to go see the lobby again and mingle with the crowds. Do you know, I have never seen so many modish people in one place before. I've enjoyed studying the gowns, and some of the men are as dandified as the Beau himself." She turned to her aunt. "Do you wish to join us?"

"No, I'm quite comfortable here. I'll simply rest awhile and enjoy the view. A cup of punch does sound interesting, however."

"Then you shall have a cup within minutes. I'll send it up by an usher while we stroll around and visit. I've spied several of my acquaintances in the audience and would like to speak to them." Lord Whitfield bowed to Maude and extended his arm to Lila. "Come along, my dear. I'm delighted to see you enjoying yourself so much. Are you glad you came?"

"Oh, yes." Lila couldn't keep the excitement from her voice. She hated to sound like a school girl on her first outing, but in reality it was almost the case. She and her father had not been able to afford the opera more than a few times, and then most often after he had won at cards. Therefore she had spent a part of her night worrying about what would happen on her father's next night of gambling, for invariably one good day of luck would be followed by a long stretch of bad. And even though she was reluctant to admit it, she was enjoying Lord Whitfield's company.

They descended the stairs slowly and joined the others who milled about in the lower lobby. Whitfield went off to purchase their punch while Lila stood by one of the huge Ionic pillars and surveyed the audience. She loved the sounds around her, the rustling of silk gowns, the tinkle of glasses and the excited chatter of theater-goers laughing and greeting friends. Even the smells were different. Mingled scents of jasmine, exotic spice from the Orient, and sweet lilac drifted her way.

"Miss Appleby, so good to see you here tonight. I didn't know you were coming. You never mentioned it to us," cried Hortense, moving to Lila's side. Her mother followed and nodded her greeting, scanning Lila's appearance as though hunting for some flaw. She did not seem nearly so glad as her daughter to see Lila.

"I . . . I wasn't sure today that I'd be able to make the performance, so I didn't mention it. Although," Lila added, "I really didn't know you were coming, either." Before the girl could ask too many questions, Lila quickly complimented her on her gown. "That's a lovely Paris style, isn't it? Is it that new shade of plum we've been reading about in *La Belle Assemblée*?"

"Yes, Papa bought it for me on his last trip to France. But I don't want to talk about me. Who are you here with? I know you didn't come alone, and you seem to be waiting for someone. Is there a secret beau that Idelia, Jacinda and I should know about? You're really the secretive one. Confess now," teased Hortense, who was in remarkably good spirits. Leaning closer, she held her fan in front of her face, and whispered, "You haven't seen anything of that handsome Lord Whitfield, have you? I so hoped he'd be here this evening, but there's such a crush you can't find a soul."

Lila didn't know what to answer, because Hortense now considered Lord Whitfield to be her personal property, even though he had scarcely showed her more attention at the tea than he had the others. But before Lila could speak, Lord Whitfield was at her side, holding two glasses of punch.

"Hello, Miss Penkridge, so good to see you here this evening. And this must be your mother." Introductions were quickly made, and Mrs. Penkridge greeted him coolly. He handed Lila a cup of punch and turned back to the Penkridges. "Will one of you have my cup and I'll go purchase two more?"

Hortense's face turned crimson and she glared at Lila. "You're here with Lord Whitfield?" she blurted out, even though her mother gave her an obvious jab in the ribs. "Now I understand why you didn't mention it to us." Her lips quivered, tears rushing to her eyes, and she whirled to leave. "Come along, Mother. It's almost curtain time and we don't want to be late."

Lila stood in stunned silence. She was afraid Lord Whitfield would ask what it was all about, but before he had time, someone called his name.

Lila took a quick sip of the sweet liquid in her cup, trying to moisten her dry throat. She was worried over what her appearance here tonight with Lord Whitfield was going to do to her school. Hortense was definitely smitten with his lordship, and Lila would now be viewed as a major rival, although this was far from correct. Couldn't she even have one night of happiness without the responsibilities of her school looming in her mind? She sighed and turned to face the person who had called out to Lord Whitfield again.

"Hugh, darling, so good to see you. Where have you been hiding, you rascal? I know you haven't been to the gaming tables in days because I've asked around about you." The speaker was a gorgeous woman in a spectacular empire-waisted gown of thin gold muslin over a petticoat of gold silk. She placed her hand on Lord Whitfield's arm in a most personal manner while she scanned Lila curiously.

Lila struggled to meet her gaze with a soft smile and not squirm or blush. It was evident the woman thought her of little or no competition for Lord Whitfield's attentions.

"Miss Appleby, I'd like for you to meet the Duchess of Halstead." Lord Whitfield smiled at the other woman and said, "Duchess, this is Miss Lila Appleby. She is my next door neighbor and runs a school for young ladies."

Lila curtsied and said, "Your Grace, so pleased to meet you," which was not entirely true, but the necessary response nonetheless.

"How quaint," replied the duchess, coolly turning back to Whitfield. She let Lila know that she had little time to be bothered with a commoner of her ilk.

Lila stood quietly, trying not to listen as they chatted. She studied the duchess's daring dress. The square neckline was cut scandalously low. Around her slender neck nestled a diamond necklace with a large diamond pendant that dropped into the swell of her bosom, accenting her cleavage. The duchess wore her raven hair in the most modish of new styles, its curls shorn short and held into place by a band of diamonds and pearls.

Since the duchess continued to monopolize Lord Whitfield's attention and thwarted every attempt he made to include Lila in the conversation, Lila felt at liberty to ignore them and scan the crowd. She spotted Hortense and her mother at the far end of the lobby engrossed in conversation with Lord Haydon, who looked in her direction from time to time.

Finally a bellman passed through the lobby ringing his handbell, warning the patrons that the second act was about to begin. Whitfield took Lila by the arm and said, "It's time for us to be getting back to our seats." And to the duchess, he added, "Shall we go back upstairs?"

The duchess shook her head. "No, my party is waiting for me. I simply wanted to come over, Hugh darling, and tell you that I've chosen you for my partner for the races this weekend."

Whitfield appeared about to decline, but the duchess placed her hand possessively on his arm and said, "Darling, you simply can't let me down. The Prince will be there himself, and I've already entered our names." Totally ignoring Lila, she continued, "Come by for tea tomorrow afternoon and I'll fill you in on all the details. Now, I simply won't take no for an answer."

Whitfield chuckled and said, "We'll discuss this later."

On their trip back to their box, Lila asked, "Was the duchess's husband with her?"

"No, she's a widow. The duke was quite old when she married him, and His Grace died of a stroke before they celebrated their second wedding anniversary."

"Such a shame."

"Don't feel sorry for Alana. She hasn't been the grieving widow since the duke's funeral." Seeing Lila's shock, he explained, "It was a marriage of convenience. The old duke's only son was killed in a hunting accident, and he remarried hoping to have an heir to inherit his vast holdings."

"And do they have a son?"

"Yes, the young duke was born within the first year. So the duke bestowed a fortune in jewels on Alana for making him so happy. So, my dear, all was not lost in the marriage, even if it was loveless." He sighed. "As so many marriages among the upper class are."

"I'd never marry for other than love," said Lila emphatically.

"I tend to feel that way myself, which probably explains why I'm still a bachelor well past my prime."

"You are not past your prime, my lord." Lila couldn't resist saying this. "I'd never think of you as old."

He took her arm and led her into their box. Leaning closer, he whispered, "You don't know what a comfort it is to discover that you do not find me an ancient specimen."

She was about to protest when she saw the twinkle in his eyes. He had been toying with her all along.

They returned to their seats just as the music began, so she was saved from having to comment again. Lila was grateful for the distraction, because her spirits had plummeted.

If the duchess was widowed, she must be pursuing Lord Whitfield for her next husband. The intimate glances the two had exchanged alerted Lila that they were on very personal terms. And the proprietary way the duchess had touched Lord Whitfield's arm led her to understand their relationship. No, if the duchess wanted to marry Lord Whitfield, then she, Lila, was wasting her time dreaming that he might be interested in her, a poor teacher—and plain in the bargain. The second half of the opera was not nearly so exciting for her.

On the way home she scarcely uttered a word. Aunt Maude nudged her in the ribs several times, trying to spur her into conversation, but she ignored the hints. What was the use? She didn't stand a chance with someone as handsome as Lord Whitfield. No, she simply would end this friendship now, before she suffered an even more painful broken heart. The longer she allowed herself to dream, the harder it would be to accept his marriage to the duchess. In Lila's mind there was no question but the match would take place—the duchess was too beautiful and rich to be ignored, and Lord Whitfield was so handsome and charming that any woman would want to be married to him.

When they reached home, Lord Whitfield stepped from the carriage and offered Lila his arm. They walked silently up to the front door, while Maude followed behind the couple at a discreet distance, but Lila did not utter another word.

"You seem so quiet. Did you not enjoy the opera?" Lord Whitfield asked, his face clearly showing his puzzlement.

"Oh, to the contrary. It was magnificent. I am so happy that you persuaded me to go."

"Then why, my pet, the long face?" He tickled her chin and made her smile. She gazed up into his deep brown eyes, where she felt she could drown.

The most exciting night of Lila's life had been transformed into her saddest. She realized how much happier she had been before she had fallen in love with Lord Whitfield. Now she would have to bear the pain of losing him to the Duchess of Halstead. And losing Lord Whitfield made her loss of Edward Nelson seem trivial.

Chapter 10

THE FOLLOWING DAY Lila arose with renewed determination not to think about Lord Whitfield. Having made this decision, she set about her daily chores, dressing in a simple brown gown and pulling her hair once more back into a bun at the nape of her neck. Even she frowned when she looked in the mirror and saw the prim matron who stared back at her.

She didn't want to be this woman! She wanted to be young, carefree—and in love. Finally she removed all the combs from her hair and let it flow freely down to her shoulders in soft cascading curls. Her hair was one of her best assets, and she decided the thick mane made her feel younger at least. But not wanting to lose her image as a school mistress, she compromised by tying back the locks with a rich brown velvet ribbon. The sparrow might be gone, she decided, but she still wasn't a swan.

Now, the duchess was definitely a swan. Lila felt she

was always destined to love the wrong men. Edward had married a rich woman, even though she was not beautiful, so Lila reasoned Lord Whitfield could never turn down the charms of the Duchess of Halstead who was wealthy and ravishingly beautiful. She sighed at her plight in life and stood to go down to breakfast with her aunt.

No sooner had Lila poured sugar in her tea than Aunt Maude began to scold her. "Young lady, what got into you last night?"

"I can't imagine what you're talking about," said Lila, concentrating on stirring her tea to avoid facing her aunt, because she had been expecting this lecture. "Does it look like rain today?"

"Don't try changing the subject on me, young lady. Remember, I'm your aunt and I know all your tricks. I also know that something happened last night which changed you from the lovely young lady you are into a shy mouse. What caused you to grow so quiet? I nearly had apoplexy trying to think of enough things to talk about on the ride home to prevent Lord Whitfield thinking we were rude ingrates." Maude set down her tea cup and faced Lila. "You were having such a grand time, and I was so proud of you, and then you returned from the intermission sulking like a scalded cat."

"Oh, Aunt Maude, I was not sulking. You love to overdramatize things. I was . . . was . . ." She floundered, trying to say the right thing without telling too much. "I was merely tired."

"Tired? Tired at the age of twenty-one?" Maude shook her head. "Nonsense, child. You could have danced until dawn. I know that I did many a morning when I was your age. No, it was definitely something else. Didn't you enjoy Lord Whitfield's company? Did he make a rude proposition when you were alone with him?" She studied her niece closely. There was a slight blush rising in Lila's cheeks. "I can't believe His Lordship would do such a thing! He didn't try to seduce you with hundreds of people standing around, did he?"

Lila laughed and reached for a croissant, which she gave all her attention as she buttered it and heaped raspberry jam on top. "Don't tease me this morning. I'm not in the mood for it." She took a bite and chewed carefully, trying to think of an answer that would satisfy her aunt, without explaining her true pain. Finally she said, "Lord Whitfield was a perfect gentleman. I had a wonderful time at the opera. The music and even the theatre were more than I'd hoped they'd be. So now, stop fretting and let's hurry and finish. I want to do some work on our household accounts before the girls arrive. Most of the bills are looking better, now that the girls' tuition payments are coming in weekly." Lila took a final sip of her tea and rose from the table.

"I'm not budging from this table until you answer the question you're avoiding. What happened downstairs during the intermission that caused you to look so sad when you returned to your seat? I saw the look of pain in your eyes, and I want to know why, so you might as well tell me now or I shall sit here until luncheon." Maude crossed her arms and gave Lila her most obstinate look. "You are wearing my patience thin," she warned. "And I'd hate to have to ask Lord Whitfield about the matter."

"Oh, Aunt Maude, you'd never do that, would you?" A stricken expression swept over Lila's features. "That would be the most awful of things to do." She shook her head vigorously. "It wouldn't do at all to ask Lord Whitfield, because he probably didn't even notice how quiet I grew."

"Then something did happen?" Maude nodded. "I knew it. I could tell by the way you walked when you entered the box. You looked like a whipped puppy. It was a look of absolute dejection."

"Do you think Lord Whitfield noticed?" Lila stared at her aunt, hoping that her fears wouldn't be confirmed.

"He couldn't have missed the change in behavior. Whether he was able to understand what caused it, I'm not certain, since I can't pry from you what the whole story is."

Finally, Lila sat back down and faced her aunt. "While we were downstairs the most gorgeous woman came over and began chatting with Lord Whitfield. The Duchess of Halstead. Have you ever seen her?"

"No, but I've heard much about her from acquaintances." Maude smiled and nodded as things began to grow clearer. "She's a beauty, I've heard, and has a reputation to match the king's mistress. In fact, she may have been one. I hear she's been most other men of nobility's lover." Maude had always spoken frankly to her niece. She didn't hold with keeping young women completely ignorant of the ways of the world. "So now I understand. You think Lord Whitfield might be infatuated with her and you can't compete?"

Lila grinned, because she did love her aunt so much.

The older woman had always understood her better than anyone else, and Lila was so grateful to have her as a friend as well as a relative. "That's it, Aunt Maude. If you had seen the duchess, you'd understand why I know there's no point in my being interested in Lord Whitfield. If she sets her cap for him, then the contest is over."

"How did he react to her?"

"I'm certain they are already close." Lila groped for the proper words to describe their relationship. "I'd say they're probably lovers. You should have seen the proprietary way she put her hand on his arm and stood close to him. She also told him that she had chosen him to ride for her at the races this weekend. So, I'm sure she is interested in him." Lila stood. "I must go back to my school and home problems. Let's move into the parlor, and I'll work on my books until the girls arrive."

"I forgot to mention to you that I'm paying a visit to Lady Glassford this morning. She sent her card around yesterday and asked that I drop in to see her. You remember we went to school together, and I haven't been to see her since I arrived in London. So I plan to drop by for tea this morning, and if she invites me for luncheon, I shan't return until early afternoon."

"Have a wonderful time," said Lila moving off. "I can tell you think my cause is hopeless, since you didn't comment after hearing about the duchess."

"Nonsense. I simply need time to think this thing through. Lord Whitfield seemed charmed with your company last evening, and I certainly haven't given up on him as a suitor for your hand. Now stop fretting and go do your books. Let's see what comes of last evening. He may send his card around and invite you for another outing. You must simply be patient."

It surprised Lila that after sharing her fears with Maude she felt better and not nearly so dejected. Perhaps she had overreacted to the duchess last evening.

Putting the issue aside she worked on her household accounts until she heard the chatter of the girls coming up the front steps. Sighing deeply, she closed her ledger and went to greet them, ready for another day of less than exciting teaching. She had grown quite fond of all three of the girls, each so different that Lila had to stay alert to keep ahead of them. But her favorite was probably her most taxing student, Jacinda. Miss Kingsbury was a dear girl, but filled with devilment. She spent hours thinking of ways to divert Lila from the chore she had been assigned, teaching them to be young ladies of society.

"Good morning, girls," said Lila in greeting as she stepped aside for them to enter. "You do seem in great spirits this morning."

"Oh, we are! It's a great morning, don't you think?" sang Jacinda, moving gracefully into the hallway, untying the ribbons on her bonnet.

Lila eyed the girl cautiously because it was a damp, rainy morning with little hint of sun. "You're certainly in a pleasant mood today. I hope your enthusiasm carries over into your school work."

"A pox on school work." Jacinda made an ugly face. "Let's hear about Hortense's visit to the opera. I'd far rather hear about that adventure. I don't know why my parents are so boorish that they won't take me too.

I absolutely pleaded to be included last evening, but no, they sent me to my room for disobey—" Jacinda stopped abruptly and glanced around the room nervously, then giggled. "Oh, what does it matter? You're all my friends. What fun is a secret if you can't confide it to your closest chums?"

Lila felt a warning, knowing how skilled Jacinda was at distracting the group from their work. "Young lady, you will have to wait until tea time to share this bit of chatter. You were sent here to study and we will do exactly that. Now, Hortense, please go to the piano and play the piece I assigned to you Monday." Glancing around at the others, she added, "Ladies, find a comfortable seat because our recital shall begin. I hope that you have memorized your waltz, Jacinda, because you will be next."

"I've learned mine," voiced Idelia. "At fourteen there isn't much else to do. It's either listen to my sister mooning around about Lord Whitfield or practice my piano."

"Oh, do tell us more, Idelia," begged Jacinda.

"Enough girls, back to your music." Lila tapped her baton gently on the edge of the piano to hush them.

"Miss Appleby, I simply can't concentrate on my music piece until I've asked Hortense one question. Was Lord Haydon at the opera?"

Lila gave up and threw up her hands in mock despair. "All right, we'll discuss last evening for ten minutes, but not a second longer. And," she warned, "the time shall come from the lunch break. I'll expect every girl rested and back in this room by ten of two. Agreed?"

"Yes, Miss Appleby," came the chorus.

"Now, Hortense, tell us if you saw Lord Haydon at the opera." Jacinda sat down and patted the seat beside her, inviting Hortense to join her on the settee.

"I not only saw him, but he came over and spoke with my mother and me." Hortense smiled smugly.

Jacinda's hand flew to her mouth. "You don't mean it? What did he say? Did he mention me?"

"Yes, he asked where the lovely Miss Kingsbury was."

Idelia and Jacinda giggled and clapped their hands excitedly. "And what did you tell him?" asked Jacinda, her eyes twinkling with excitement.

Hortense shrugged and thought for a moment. "Simply that Miss Kingsbury had another engagement for the evening and couldn't accompany me as previously planned."

The three girls whooped with laughter, until Lila cut in. "Girls, you didn't arrange for Jacinda to rendezvous with Lord Haydon during the opera, did you?" From the looks on all three girls' faces she knew that was exactly what they had planned. "Jacinda Kingsbury, I shall have to tell your mother if you continue to try and make assignations with Lord Haydon. Your mother made it clear to me that you were going through a headstrong age and you were not to be allowed any male companionship without the strictest of supervision. How did you girls plot this meeting?"

"Well, it never took place, Miss Appleby, so you needn't look so worried," said Hortense. "And my mother would have been present. So you see, we really weren't doing anything underhanded."

"That's a matter of opinion, my dear." Shaking her head in defeat, Lila conceded, "But I suppose no harm was really done, since the Kingsburys didn't allow Jacinda to accompany you. But you girls must be more careful in the future. A girl's reputation is her most precious asset."

"Yes, Miss Appleby," they chorused, because this was not a new lecture to any of them.

"I simply must tell the most surprising news of the evening," cried Hortense, clapping her hands to get their attention. Eyeing Miss Appleby, she leaned close and said, "Miss Appleby was at the concert and—" Holding them in suspense for a few seconds, she grinned. "—and she was accompanied by the handsome Lord Whitfield."

The girls gasped and all turned to stare at Lila.

"Now girls, we've chattered on for far too long. It's time to begin our lessons."

"You said ten minutes, and we've one minute left," argued Idelia. "I want to hear about Lord Whitfield."

"There's a simple explanation and not the one you are all hoping for. Lord Whitfield is our neighbor, and he invited my aunt and me strictly as a neighborly gesture." Lila saw the looks of disappointment on the girls' faces. "Sorry to disappoint you, but that's all there is to the story." She did not miss Hortense's look of relief, so she felt compelled to add a warning. "And none of you need be setting your caps for Lord Whitfield. I think there are many young bucks in London who are more what your mamas have in mind for you." She clapped her hands. "Now, this is your last warning. Hortense, begin your piece. Not another word is to be uttered until tea time or I shall add more scales for homework tonight."

The girls knew when they had pushed their teacher to the limit, thus they fell silent and listened as Hortense struggled through her piano piece.

To Lila's relief they did not broach the subject of Lord Whitfield again and the rest of the morning continued uneventfully. It was not until the girls had finished their afternoon French lessons that Maude rushed in all aflutter.

"Lila, girls, I apologize for interrupting—"

Lila glanced up, startled to see her aunt so flustered and excited. "That's all right, we're almost finished for the day. What happened, Aunt Maude. Are you ill?"

"Were you in an accident?" cried Idelia, jumping up from her chair and rushing over.

Maude shook her head vigorously. "No, no, nothing like that. I have wonderful news. Just give me a minute to catch my breath after that climb up the steps and I'll tell everyone."

They all crowded around while Maude let the excitement build, and then she began. "You know, Lila, my good friend Lady Glassford married well and Lord Glassford owned a box in Vauxhall. Since his death she hasn't used it much, and this season she plans to travel to Manchester to visit with her daughter, who is expecting her first child, so she offered her box to us for the Season." She looked into Lila's startled face. "Free! Not a shilling would she take, although I offered to rent it."

Lila's expression relaxed, and she began to feel the excitement of the others. "How wonderful! Girls, do you want to go to Vauxhall next week? The gardens are beautiful this time of year. What a lovely thing for Lady Glassford to do. After our trip we must all write her a letter and thank her for her generosity."

"Lady Glassford was so impressed by the work you're doing, Lila. She wanted to know all the details. Afterwards she volunteered the use of her box. She said that she admired a young woman of independence and wished she were younger, so she might try such a venture herself." Maude laughed. "Although I can't imagine her doing anything other than entertaining with her famous house parties and crushes."

"Imagine having our very own private box. I wonder who will be on each side of us? It could be the Prince Regent for all we know." Hortense grinned impishly. "Do you think we should brush up on our royal titles before our visit?"

They all had a laugh over that. The excitement was contagious and Lila felt her spirits soaring until she asked the next question. "Did she happen to mention who we are near?"

"As a matter of fact, she did. And you'll never believe who it is. Anyone care to guess?"

"No, but tell us immediately. It's almost time for our carriages and we must know every detail so we can tell our mamas," said Hortense. "Oh, Mama is going to be so thrilled. Miss Appleby, yours is the best school in London."

"Aunt Maude, don't torture us another moment. Now, share the name with us, please." Lila knew her aunt must have very exciting news to look so flushed.

"Lord Whitfield." Maude's eyes sparkled as she

spoke and she looked directly at Lila. "Now isn't that the best of luck?"

Lila felt herself grow cold. All the fun had gone out of the outing for her. Suppose Lord Whitfield was there, and with the Duchess of Halstead. It would be an absolutely disastrous experience and one she did not care to experience. But a look around at all the eager faces told her that she simply couldn't disappoint her girls or Aunt Maude. She'd have to make the best of it.

Hortense squealed with delight and clapped her hand together. "I think it is wonderful."

"So do I," chimed in Jacinda. "I wonder if he'll be using his box next week when we're there?"

"You don't care a whit about seeing Lord Whitfield," teased Idelia. "You just want to see Lord Haydon."

"Well, what if I do?" sniffed Jacinda, sticking out her tongue at Idelia. "Sometimes Idelia, you're such a sap skull."

"Girls! Girls! Stop this bickering. We act like ladies here at all times and that means no name calling, do you understand?" Lila glanced at the clock and stood. It was almost time for their classes to end for the day, and not a minute too soon. She needed time alone to digest this upcoming event and what it might entail.

"Yes, Miss Appleby," they said in unison.

"Now get your wraps. Classes are dismissed for today. We have a week to discuss our trip. But first all must go home and check with their mothers. We can't go if any mother objects."

"Nobody's mama could object to this wonderful opportunity," said Hortense.

"And Jacinda, you behave this next week so your mother will let you go. It's not the time to get sent to your room or have all your privileges taken away." Lila handed Jacinda her yellow bonnet.

"What shall we do about a picnic?" asked Idelia, putting away her sheet music and going to sit down.

"Lady Glassford advised me to pack a picnic lunch at home and take it. She said prices are ridiculous. Why the other day she paid eleven shillings for a small portion of ham and two tiny chickens," put in Maude.

"I'll ask Papa for a bottle of wine. He just got a case from France this week," volunteered Jacinda.

"Then we'll tell Mama to have Cook pack us some cold meats and cheese," said Hortense.

"I don't want to impose," said Lila.

"Miss Appleby, Mama will be so excited for us that she won't mind at all." Hortense looked around for her tablet. "I'll write down the things we're to take."

"If your mothers agree to this, then I'll have Cook bake some of her biscuits and her famous spice cake. I think it's going to be an exciting outing for all of us." There was a sudden sharp clap of thunder and all looked out the window. "Let's hope next week brings us a sunny Thursday."

At the sound of carriages approaching, the girls dashed to the front door. Lila followed to the steps, waving them off. She was about to turn and go back into the house when a black carriage decorated in gold and bearing a huge crest on its door pulled up at Brighton Hall. Before she could turn to go inside, Lord Whitfield stepped from the coach and turned to face her. He smiled up at Lila and nodded in greeting. She was about to wave in return when the Duchess of Halstead stepped from the coach and took Lord Whitfield's arm.

The duchess turned to see what Whitfield was staring at, and when she saw Lila, her smile faded. She frowned, ignored Lila, and turned back to Whitfield.

Whirling, Lila retreated into her house, the excitement of the past hour totally destroyed by what she'd just witnessed.

Lila closed the door and leaned against it, battling to keep the tears from flowing. She didn't think her heart could stand to be broken again. Edward had meant nothing to her compared to the emotions she felt for Lord Whitfield. She had known better than to fall for the earl's charms. Hadn't she been the first to say he was untameable?

Trying to convince herself that it really didn't matter, Lila threw herself into plans for the following Thursday's outing.

Chapter 11

ON THE APPOINTED day for the group's trip to Vauxhall Gardens, rain fell in the morning, but even the thunder and lightning couldn't dampen everyone's spirits. Rain was so common in London that the girls knew a morning gale could easily give way to a beautiful sunny afternoon or a cloudless night, which is exactly what happened on this day.

All the girls had agreed to be ready by eight in the evening, so that they might be in their box before the orchestra began playing. Hortense and Idelia's parents were so thrilled over their going that Mr. Penkridge had volunteered his coach to the group, much to Lila's relief, for this saved the expense of a hackney.

The girls drew up at the Appleby residence on the dot of half past seven. Lila and Maude waited with brimming picnic baskets. The Kingsbury coach had been sent along to pick up Nettie and Rose, who would serve the meal and clear away afterwards. The two servants stood waiting, as excited as the others, because everyone had heard of the famous gardens.

Lila had seen Lord Whitfield depart from his house earlier that evening, and she wondered where he might be off to so early. There were so many events taking place all over London during the Season that it was impossible to even attempt a guess.

"Now girls, when we get to the gates, does everyone have her fare for admission? It's three shillings, and if you left your money home, I have enough for everyone." Lila looked at the excited girls. They were lovely tonight in their rainbow of colored gowns, and the excitement added a rosy hue to their fair cheeks.

Lila had chosen a medium blue gown that didn't show too much wear and that Maude had doctored with a few sprigs of white lilies and bluebells made of silk. Aunt Maude looked the role of wealthy matron this evening, dressed in purple taffeta with her white hair swept up and held in place with ivory combs. Yes, as Lila surveyed her group, she felt pleased. They were as attractive a group as would be at the gardens.

The coach traveled north on Kensington Lane and to the west entrance of the gardens. Coaches were pulling up and crowds were entering as they approached the gates.

Once inside they strolled down the tree-lined walkway until they came to their box. Lady Glassford had given Maude explicit instructions, so they traveled down the main walkway with an air of confidence. No one would have guessed it was their first visit to the gardens.

"Good evening, Miss Appleby," came a familiar

voice from behind Lila. She turned to face Lord Whitfield and her heart gave an unexpected lurch. It annoyed her when it did such unreasonable things—didn't it understand that Lord Whitfield was beyond her grasp just as Edward had been? Only in Lord Whitfield's case he was too rich to marry a poor girl like her, yet he seemed to take pleasure in turning up at odd moments and toying with her emotions.

"Good evening, my lord. I didn't expect to see you here tonight. Do you come here often?" She was chattering like a silly goose, and it was all because he rattled her so with that charming smile. Why did he have to be so dashing? She tried to maintain her poise.

"We're here on an outing and it's so thrilling. This is the first time Hortense, Jacinda, and I have visited the gardens," chimed in Idelia.

"In that case, why not let me escort you ladies around?" Lord Whitfield appeared delighted to see the group. "I tell you what, I have a small party in my box, but why don't the five of you come join us. I'll order more wine and food. We'll have a splendid time of it. The concert tonight is supposed to be one of Mr. James Hook's finest arrangements."

The girls all turned to Lila, appealing to her to agree, but she shook her head, declining the invitation politely. "Thank you so much for your kind offer, but we have a box for the evening. Lady Glassford is a dear friend of my aunt's and has graciously consented for us to use hers for the evening."

"What a splendid coincidence! It is next to mine. We shall be able to enjoy the concert and visit too." Lord

Whitfield held out his arm to Maude and said, "Mrs. Watson, allow me to escort you to the boxes, if I may."

Lila and the girls trailed behind, Lila feeling a twinge of envy that it was Aunt Maude on Whitfield's arm rather than her. Such nonsense, she scolded herself, simply had to stop. She attributed this romantic feeling to the atmosphere around her. The gardens were ablaze with roses, tulips, and flowering shrubs. And while the night air was a bit cool, her pelisse was sufficient cover against the slight breeze. All in all it was a pleasant English evening and she was in high spirits.

However, when they reached their boxes, Lord Whitfield insisted they come over to his and meet his party. As Lila feared, the Duchess of Halstead was among his dinner guests, along with Lord Haydon and a third gentleman, introduced as Sir Nigel Cunnington.

Lord Haydon's face brightened when he saw Jacinda, and he stood to greet them. "Miss Kingsbury, how nice to see you again." He took her hand and kissed it, while Jacinda smiled up at him charmingly. They chatted quietly while Whitfield introduced the others.

It was evident that the duchess was less than pleased to see Lila again. She nodded curtly and then returned to studying the glass of champagne she twirled slowly between her fingers. After the amenities had been passed, the duchess moved to Whitfield's side, sliding her hand under his arm and looking up at him with a pout on her face. "Darling Hugh, you promised me a stroll around the gardens before the concert, and it will start soon."

"But we have guests here now, my dear . . ." Whitfield remained polite, but he removed her hand from his arm.

"By all means, go right ahead," jumped in Lila. "We don't want to keep you from your planned evening." Turning to her group, she said, "Come along, girls. We must get settled in our box before the concert begins. I don't want to miss a minute of it. I've heard Mr. Hook's compositions are fabulous."

Lila saw that Lord Whitfield did not want them to leave, but she could not get away from the duchess fast enough to suit her. For some reason, the woman did not like her, either. Perhaps it was because she was not titled, but somehow she doubted that. It was only a supposition, but Lila felt the duchess was jealous of the attention Lord Whitfield paid to her, although why the woman should feel that way was a mystery to her.

Lila's party moved back to their box where Nettie and Rose had set up the picnic. The boxes were all beautifully decorated with paintings by Francis Hayman. Rose had packed the best linen cloth to cover the furnished table. Even real crystal was used for drinking the wine Jacinda's father had sent. Just as they were sitting down to their meal of cold chicken and cheese, the musicians tuned up and the concert began. For a while Lila forgot all her money troubles and basked in how wonderful it was to be here, at Vauxhall and in her very own box.

"Miss Appleby," whispered Jacinda, who had moved over to Lila's side after the meal was finished and the maids had packed away the dishes, "may Hortense, Idelia, and I stroll around the paths for a while?"

"Don't you want to hear the concert?" asked Lila, who didn't wish to be interrupted and couldn't understand how the girls could feel otherwise.

"Oh, we've discussed it, and we can listen to the music as we stroll around. I understand it can be heard a great distance."

Lila nodded. "All right, but don't disturb the others by talking loudly."

"No, ma'am, we won't."

Before Lila could caution against anything else, the girls dashed out of the box and down the trail. There were five walkways to chose from, and the girls started down the Grand Walkway at a demure pace, holding hands and behaving very ladylike. Lila watched them until they moved out of sight, pleased with their behavior and that they seemed to be getting along so well. She began to relax as she listened to the music, knowing there was little trouble for the girls to get into here in the park where the walkways were well lighted and large groups strolled together, nodding politely as they passed and repassed during their promenade.

For the next hour and a half Lila forgot she was a teacher and sat back to enjoy the enchantment of the evening. Even Lord Whitfield failed to compete for her thoughts as she hummed along with the selections she recognized.

Lila had seen Lord Whitfield and the duchess stroll by on their way to the nature paths. It had only amused her when shortly before the concert ended the couple had returned and the duchess chose to lean up and kiss Lord Whitfield lightly on his cheek just as they passed Lila's box. Lila realized the duchess had done this for her benefit, but even that had not ruffled her tranquil happiness. A slight moment of acute jealousy and a strong urge to box the duchess's ears, and then, the feeling was gone. See, she was learning to control her emotions, she thought smugly.

Finally the concert ended and Lila opened her eyes lazily, for the wine had lulled her into a warm contentment.

"Rose and Nettie, gather our belongs, we'd better be getting home. I don't want to keep the girls out too late or their parents might not consent for them to come again." She smiled at her aunt and said, "This has been the most wonderful evening. Shall we take a stroll through the pathways before we depart?"

"I think that is a splendid idea. After eating so much late supper, I need to move around a little before retiring. Besides, I'm looking forward to seeing the flowers."

So the two started off on their leisurely stroll. "I wonder where the girls are?" asked Lila after they had walked down the South Walkway. I thought we might pass them at some point and I'd be able to tell them to head back to the box so we can begin to gather our things together."

"Oh, we'll catch up with them on one of the paths," said Maude confidently, taking Lila's arm to steady her step on the graveled path.

But when they had toured four of the walkways from the Grand to the South without any sign of the girls, Lila began to grow uneasy. "Where do you suppose they could be?" She glanced around her nervously. Surely nothing could have happened to them. Suddenly she gasped and said, "You don't suppose those imps went down the Dark Walk, do you? I've heard that it's also called the Lover's Walk and young rakes are known to draw ladies into the bushes and kiss them."

"That sounds like where you might find Jacinda," said Maude, looking through the crowd, searching for some sign of the girls' colorful outfits. "Wait," she said, touching Lila's arm. "I think I caught a glimpse of Hortense's lavender gown and purple pelisse."

"Where?" Lila's spirits rose as she strained to follow her aunt's gaze.

"Yes, that's Hortense. Quickly, come along. Let's catch up with them before they move out of sight." Walking briskly they made their way through the crowd until they were within twenty feet of the girls.

The girls had paused at the Grand Crosswalk as though debating which direction to go next, and Lila hailed them, waving for them to wait. "I don't see Jacinda," she said as they neared the girls.

"She can't be far away," said Maude, although she wasn't at all sure about this. There was no need to spoil Lila's evening until it was necessary.

"Girls, where is Jacinda?" Lila paused to catch her breath and to help Maude to a bench where she could rest a moment. Fanning herself with a handkerchief, Lila looked from one sister to the other. "I asked you where Jacinda is."

"We ran into Lord Haydon and Jacinda walked with him. When Idelia and I looked around, we didn't see them anymore. I suppose we took different paths," said Hortense innocently.

"How long have they been gone?" cried Lila, feeling the responsibility of Jacinda's reputation lay on her shoulders, although she had grown to suspect the girl's wild behavior was nothing new to her parents.

"We really don't know, Miss Appleby," replied Hortense. "As I said before, we were walking ahead of them, and when we looked back they were gone."

"Aunt Maude you take the girls back to the box, and I'll go find Jacinda. I'll be along with her shortly. The park doesn't close until two in the morning, so we have plenty of time to find them. I'll check back at the box after every circle."

Lila headed off toward the path, hoping to catch a glimpse of Jacinda's colorful bonnet in the crowd. Tonight Jacinda had worn a beautiful yellow velvet bonnet with a large white plume, so it should be easy to spot once she was on the correct path. But after Lila had circled the four paths and returned to the box where the others waited, she began to grow anxious. There was only one walkway left, and it was the Lover's Walk.

Standing straight, Lila started down the trail. It was not a frightening path, since crime was not a problem here, but merely dark and romantic for couples in love. It was the most popular walkway, and the one most likely to entice Jacinda and Lord Haydon.

LORD WHITFIELD HAD seen Lila pass in front of his box, and had also seen her leave again alone and in a great hurry. Seeing that Lord Haydon had also disappeared, he suspected that Haydon and Lila might be meeting secretly and discovered a strange pang of jealousy.

Whitfield didn't understand why he felt possessive of Lila when she meant absolutely nothing to him, yet he stood and followed her, planning to confirm his suspicions. When she started down the dark Lover's Walk, he quickened his step, more confident than ever that she was off to a clandestine meeting with someone. He could imagine Lila's falling into Haydon's arms and felt he should warn her that the man was likely to be toying with her affections. Never did he stop to think were this actually the situation that it was of absolutely no concern of his. Instead, for some strange reason, he took on a proprietary role where Lila was involved.

Lila heard footsteps behind her but didn't turn to investigate. The path frightened her a bit, and she grew annoyed with Jacinda for forcing her to come here alone. Perhaps she should have brought Aunt Maude with her, or even asked Lord Whitfield to accompany her. But, she realized the duchess would have put up an argument had Lord Whitfield deserted her side to search for a wayward chit. Ahead Lila saw a couple embracing in what appeared to be a passionate kiss, so she speeded up her step. It might be Jacinda and Haydon.

Walking briskly up to the couple, Lila called, "Jacinda? Is that you?" The couple sprang apart and she gasped. The girl looked nothing like Jacinda and the man glared at her angrily. "I am so sorry," she mumbled as she backed away and continued her journey down the pathway.

Suddenly from out of the dark there came a low chuckle and a hand reached out and seized Lila's arm. She screamed loudly as she was dragged toward the shrubs, fighting furiously.

"Take your hands off the lady," came a brisk command from behind Lila.

To her relief she was released, and she fell back into the arms of the speaker. "My dear, are you all right?"

"Lord Whitfield, thank heavens it's you. I've never been so terrified by anything." Lila clung to him in the darkness, resting her head on his comforting shoulder, savoring the feeling of his strong arms holding her close.

Lord Whitfield stroked her shoulder reassuringly, amazed at how much he enjoyed the feel of her skin beneath his hand. "You are an enticing young woman, my dear," he said, drawing her even closer.

"Please, sir, you must turn me loose."

"Why?" he teased. "This is what lovers do when they come down this path."

"But we aren't lovers," she gasped, not sure she could breathe with him so close and her heart beating so rapidly.

"Then perhaps we should mend that." He leaned closer and whispered in her ear. "I have the most uncanny desire to kiss you, my dear Miss Appleby."

"Lord Whitfield, you can't be thinking of kissing me."

"But that's why you came down this path alone, isn't it? To be kissed by some stranger?" His voice grew gruff and he appeared angry. She did not understand him, and didn't know how she had given him the impression she was such a loose baggage, but she had to correct that image.

Trying to pull away from his grasp, she said, "Jacinda is missing and she's off with your friend Lord Haydon. I'm responsible for her. Can't you see this isn't the time for me to be thinking of my interests?"

"I tell you what, my dear. For the price of a kiss, I'll help you find the lovers."

Lila squirmed within his strong arms. "Why is it that every time you get alone with me, you try to kiss me? Don't you realize that is a most unchivalrous gesture?"

"I rather fancied it as a flattering gesture myself," he teased, still holding her firm.

"Please, Lord Whitfield, I must find Jacinda. She may . . . may . . ."

"I dare say that Miss Kingsbury knows exactly what she's doing at the moment and is enjoying herself greatly. Knowing Lord Haydon, I'd wager that she is safe and very content to be in his company."

Drawing Lila closer, he said, "I've wanted for some time to get you alone and kiss that pretty little mouth again. It seems to be begging to be kissed every time I glance in your direction. So why don't you stop worrying about Jacinda and listen to your own heart for a change?"

Lila felt his warmth through her pelisse, and she yearned to feel his lips against hers. Their first kiss still lingered in her memory, but what type of woman would he think her, if she did not offer some resistance?

"Unhand me this moment!" Lila twisted from his grasp. "I must find Jacinda. It's getting late and we are all due home before midnight."

"Do you turn into a pumpkin at midnight?" He chuckled to himself as he watched her temper flare.

"No, but I'd like to turn into a witch." She stamped her dainty foot. "You are the most annoying rake I've ever met."

"Have you met many?" He appeared absolutely undaunted by her flare of anger.

"Enough to know you are the worst of the lot. There's no wonder your best friend is Lord Haydon." She stormed down the path with him trailing behind.

"If you insist upon finding the lovers, then I suppose I might as well help you." He grabbed her arm as she started into a thick hedge from which giggles could be heard. "Hold up! You can't go charging in on people like that. Wait here and call out to them."

"Jacinda. Jacinda, is that you?" she called sweetly, giving Lord Whitfield a look that should have wounded a mortal man. Instead of flinching, he merely chuckled and grinned.

There was silence from the hedge. She tried again, "Jacinda, are you in there?"

"There's no one by that name here," called a gruff masculine voice.

"See," said Whitfield. "Now aren't you glad you took my advice?" They moved off down the path.

They rounded a curve in the path and there, sitting on a bench under one of the lamplights sat the lovers, deeply engrossed in conversation. They didn't even see Lila and Whitfield until they were even with them.

"Jacinda, I'm so relieved to have found you." Lila felt a rush of relief, followed by anger. "Come along, Miss Kingsbury. Our party is about to leave the park."

"Miss Appleby, I'm so sorry. The time simply got away from me. You aren't angry with me, are you?" Jacinda jumped to her feet and turned to take Haydon's hand in hers. "I must go now."

Haydon stood and bowed to Lila. "Miss Appleby, please don't be angry with Miss Kingsbury; it's all my fault. I'm the one who detained her so long." He smiled and offered his hand to Jacinda. "We had such a delightful conversation that the time flew by."

"Lord Haydon, your affairs are none of my concern; however, if you wish to walk out with Miss Kingsbury, then I suggest you visit her at her home and pay your proper respects to her parents." Lila tried not to sound like a stiff, old matron, but it was difficult to remain calm when her school and career were put in danger every time these two sneaked off together. "Come along, Jacinda, it is time for us to be going home."

Jacinda dropped Haydon's arm, gave him a soulful look, and started down the path at his side. Lila turned to follow them.

"I think it would be wise, Miss Appleby, if you allowed me to escort you back to your party," said Whitfield, offering his arm. "As I stated earlier, this is not an appropriate walk for a lady to take alone."

Lila agreed, but did not take his arm, until she tripped on the gravel on the pathway and stumbled. Whitfield caught her gracefully and steadied her. "Here, take my arm and stop being so stubborn. You are the most headstrong woman I've ever encountered."

"You do realize that you are under no obligation to stay here with me," Lila said, her face burning. "I should think the Duchess of Halstead is wondering where you are by now."

Lila had no sooner said these words than the duchess came charging toward them.

"Hugh, what is the meaning of this? I have never been so insulted in my life. One minute you're with me and the next you've gone off strolling with this . . . this . . ." The duchess groped for a word ugly enough to describe Lila, whose face flamed red under the attack. "And not once tonight, but twice. Take me home this instant or I shall call a carriage." The duchess's blue eyes blazed from Hugh to Lila, and she appeared ready to make a scene.

"Alana, that's enough. I warn you to curb your tongue or you shall regret it," said Lord Whitfield glaring back at her, his eyes smoldering, too.

"Please, please, it isn't as you might think," added Lila weakly. This was turning into a nightmare. "Please, I can accompany Jacinda and Lord Haydon back to our box. You go along with Her Grace."

"I'll do nothing of the kind," snapped Whitfield. "Alana, you owe Miss Appleby an apology. She has done nothing to deserve your wrath."

The duchess's gaze swept across Lila once more, taking in her plain gown and well-worn kidskin slippers, and then she said, just to be mean, "I should hope you would choose someone more attractive than this homely mouse to cast me aside for." With that she whirled away and started down the path, hurling one last comment over her shoulder: "I'll be waiting for you in your box, Hugh, but don't be long. I have no patience with philanderers."

"I wish you'd go along with the duchess," said Lila softly. "I can't abide scenes, yet it seems I've been the focus of several lately." She laughed. "It's ironical. Jacinda and Lord Haydon are the lovers, yet I seem to cause the greatest stir."

"Please accept my apologies for Alana's behavior. In fact, Miss Appleby, I wish to make up to you for this most embarrassing encounter. May I call for you and take you to the horse races on Saturday next to compensate for your evening being ruined?"

"I . . . I . . ." Lila stammered, speechless, unable to know how to answer. "I don't know. I mean, you really don't have to do that. I can understand the duchess's irritation at your being absent so much during your evening out." She wanted to point out that he was acting unchivalrously toward the duchess, but she bit her tongue.

"No hurry for your answer. I shall come around day after tomorrow, but you simply must let me make amends for making such a muck of this evening."

They had reached Lila's box, and Lord Whitfield took her hand and kissed it gallantly. "Until day after the morrow, then."

"Hugh, darling, don't be angry with me." The duchess's voice drifted over into Lila's box.

Lila grabbed up the picnic basket and handed it to Rose. "Come along everybody, we must be going home."

When they had departed and were on their way home, Lila finally calmed down enough to speak with Jacinda. "Bring your mother with you in the morning. I need to talk with her."

"Oh, Miss Appleby, please don't tell mother about Lord Haydon. She'll be very angry with me."

"This time, Jacinda, I have no choice but to talk with her. I cannot take the responsibility for you meeting Lord Haydon at every opportunity."

"Oh, please, Miss Appleby, don't tell my mother. That's how I got in trouble at the last school, and my mother will be furious with me."

"I regret having to do this, Jacinda, but if you are seeing a gentleman, then you need to be properly chaperoned and your mother expects me to be doing exactly that. Your parents trust me to watch after you, and I can not betray that trust. My reputation and the reputation of my school is at stake here."

The Penkridge girls gasped at the idea of Mrs. Kingsbury being contacted.

"And girls, I suggest you not carry tales home about this incident, or your parents may decide to forbid your attending future outings, which would be most grievous to us all," Lila warned the two Penkridge sisters, although she doubted they would heed her warning.

THE FOLLOWING MORNING Lila waited nervously for Mrs. Kingsbury to arrive with Jacinda. She did not know what to expect from the woman when she did appear. She had asked Mrs. Kingsbury to come early so that they might discuss the matter in privacy before the other girls arrived for classes.

When the appointed nine-thirty arrived, Lila heard a carriage pull up outside. She moved to the window where she watched Jacinda step down from the carriage, accompanied by her mother. Lila felt a faint ripple of unease, because Jacinda was smiling and laughing at something her mother said. Surprised that Jacinda seemed not the least crestfallen, Lila drew herself up straight and moved to the library to await their arrival, suddenly unsure what was about to transpire.

Lila listened as Nettie greeted the Kingsburys at the door and ushered them down the hall to the library. She heard Mrs. Kingsbury refuse to turn her coat over to the maid, so Lila knew the conference would be brief.

Jacinda, outfitted in a strawberry morning dress, breezed into the library with an air of confidence at which even Lila had to marvel. Not a tear, not a glance cast downward in shame. Instead she walked with a firm step, chin held high and a smile on her face that would charm a dowager.

Once they were seated, Lila cleared her throat, took a deep breath and said, "I suppose Jacinda told you why I asked you to accompany her this morning?" Mrs. Kingsbury nodded, but sat rigidly upright, not smiling. Lila felt certain Jacinda had already told her mother about the incident last evening, but Mrs. Kingsbury's reaction puzzled Lila.

"Miss Appleby, I have had a long discussion with Jacinda and she has related the incident as it really happened," said Mrs. Kingsbury. Turning to Jacinda, she said, "Didn't you, dear?"

"Yes, ma'am," said the young girl, who nodded, looking for the world like an innocent, which made Lila grind her teeth silently.

"I tried to stay with the group, but when I stopped to

look at some flowers, Idelia and Hortense were gone."
Jacinda's lower lip trembled as though the thought of
being left alone still frightened her. Why, the little
minx, thought Lila.

What is going on here, Lila wondered. Mrs.
Kingsbury was acting as though Lila were at fault, instead of being irate with her daughter. Lila suddenly
realized her mistake. Jacinda was skilled at manipulat-
ing her parents, and obviously had convinced them it
was all Lila's fault she had been off alone with Lord
Haydon. Gad! The girl had probably painted the man
as a saint sent from heaven to rescue her.

"My husband and I hold you responsible for our
daughter being properly chaperoned at all times, however, we are willing to give you another chance.
Jacinda has enjoyed your classes, and we've seen more
improvement here than at any of her other schools.
While we do not condone your lax supervision, Mr.
Kingsbury and I do not want to upset Jacinda, who
cried all night when she feared we might pull her out
of your school. She has agreed to tell us if you are der-
elict in your duties again. I can assure you that we will
not tolerate further shows of poor judgment."

Lila could scarce believe what she was hearing. Mrs.
Kingsbury was blaming her for everything, yet was
giving her another chance. What could she accomplish
by telling her Jacinda had bamboozled them both? The
woman simply didn't want to hear that her daughter
was wild as the wind. Lila drew a deep breath. "I will
do my best to see that Jacinda is never left unchaperoned again." That was the truth if ever she'd uttered it.

"Then the matter is closed."

"I may continue to attend your classes?" cried Jacinda, jumping to her feet and smiling broadly.

"So long as you promise to stay with the group and not wander off by yourself." What else could Lila do? She liked the girl and she needed the tuition badly.

"I'm so relieved to hear you are a reasonable person, Miss Appleby. I realize Jacinda is spoiled and headstrong, but in another year she will be old enough for her coming out, and you will have refined her . . . her, shall we say, rough edges to the point that she should make an advantageous marriage."

In Haydon's defense, Lila offered, "I suppose Lord Haydon would be a very good catch, being heir to his father's estate."

Mrs. Kingsbury shook her head. "There I'm afraid you are wrong. Mr. Kingsbury has had the gentleman investigated, and he is a known gambler who has squandered away most of his inheritance and would no doubt be delighted to marry Jacinda, commoner that she may be, because her own inheritance will be very large. We have deemed him unsatisfactory for this reason and have forbidden Jacinda to see him."

She changed her position in the chair and said in a low voice, "You see, Miss Appleby, Lord Haydon has already come calling on Mr. Kingsbury and asked for permission to pay court to Jacinda. Mr. Kingsbury denied this request after studying his lordship's jaded past." Mrs. Kingsbury leaned closer. "He also has a history of being a rake with a long list of liaisons. I hope you can understand our feeling that he is unsuitable for our Jacinda. Why, she is lovely enough, and with you expertly polishing her skills for the *ton*, she could possibly land a duke."

Lila cleared her voice. "Yes, of course. And I will do my best to see that the romance is squelched while Jacinda is in my care." Lila stood and moved toward the door. She wanted Mrs. Kingsbury to be gone before the Penkridge sisters arrived, just in case Mrs. Penkridge came storming in demanding a conference. Some days Lila wished she'd taken up being a seamstress. It had to be easier than this.

Chapter 12

THE NEXT TWO days were uneventful, with Jacinda behaving like the model young student and the lessons going so smoothly that Lila began to relax. She felt certain Jacinda had concocted some tale about her mother's visit and had shared this with Hortense and Idelia, but so long as the girls continued to behave like ladies, it was of no importance to her.

Late on the second afternoon after the girls had departed for the day, Lila decided to take a stroll in her garden. She had expected Lord Whitfield to call by afternoon tea, but so far there had not been a word from him. At least he could have sent over a note, she thought irritably.

But she had other matters on her mind. Of late she had been rather depressed over her financial situation. Although there was enough income coming in now with the girls' tuition, still the future looked less than prosperous. She'd found the best medicine for this type of problem was to stroll in her garden and enjoy the flowers, which continued to bloom and brighten the yard. After picking a rose, she idly moved over to a bench under an oak and sat down. She twirled the rose absentmindedly, smelling its sweet fragrance from time to time, and then she began plucking its petals.

"What's the verdict?" a familiar voice asked.

Lila jumped and turned to face the speaker. "Goodness, you startled me, Lord Whitfield. What are you doing here?"

"If you notice, I'm in my garden, but with your permission I'll come over and visit. You look like you could use the company."

Before waiting for her answer he opened the iron gate that separated the two yards and strolled over, taking his seat on the bench beside her.

"You haven't told me the verdict," he said.

"What are you talking about?"

"The rose. Does he love you or not?" He grinned seeing that she was still confused. "You looked like you were pulling off the petals saying, 'He loves me. He loves me not.' and I want to know the verdict."

"Oh, I wasn't doing that." She tossed the rose into the bushes. "I was thinking of something else."

"Me, I hope."

"I'm afraid not." She studied him a moment before speaking. "You are a vain rascal, aren't you? Why would I think about you?"

"If not me, then some other fortunate man. You had that faraway look on your face. Eyes glazed over. That sort of thing."

"I'm sorry to disappoint you, but I was definitely not thinking about a gentleman."

"Oh, I didn't say he was a gentleman."

Lila's face flamed. "You deliberately try to anger me, don't you? You love to taunt me. Mock me. Whatever suits your mood." She stood to leave, but he reached out and took her wrist.

"Don't go," he said softly. "I didn't mean to offend you."

"If you wish me to stay, you'll have to talk about something else."

"All right, you pick the subject."

"Did you go to Parliament today?"

"Now that's a strange thing for a woman to ask. Why, are you interested?"

"Yes, I want to know everything that happened. I . . ." She stared at the ground and kicked at a stone with the toe of her shoe. "I miss having my father to talk to about current events."

"Your aunt doesn't talk about such?"

She laughed, showing him that she really was quite lovely when she allowed herself to enjoy life. "Aunt Maude? Never. She talks about the price of knitting yarn or how many potatoes Cook put in the stew, but never what's happening in politics."

"Well, let me see."

Lila became acutely aware of the fact he had not turned her hand loose, but held it firmly while rubbing it gently with his thumb.

"Today we talked about the state of poor people in England. You know there are what we call Poor Laws which prohibit them moving out of one poor section into another."

"It's a very unfair law."

"You're probably correct. And if the people move to earn gainful employment, then nobody complains about their moving." He smiled at her. "I didn't realize you were concerned about the poor."

"Considering I'm one of them, it is of great interest to me."

"I thought you were doing well with your school."

"I'm fine for the moment, but if Lord Haydon doesn't stop trotting at Jacinda's heels, then I fear her mother will withdraw her from my school."

"Let's not talk of this anymore. Come. Let me show you something wonderful which will cheer you, I promise." He took both Lila's hands in his and pulled her to her feet. "Follow me."

She didn't want to go with him. He was his charming best this afternoon, and silently loving him was part of her problem. Still she wanted to see what he was talking about, so she followed him through the gate and into his garden.

She had only been here once before and that was to find Jacinda, so she stared around with curiosity. "The garden is well kept. Your tulips are gorgeous."

"Do you like them? I didn't have a thing to do with them. Thomas tends the gardens. He worked for my uncle and stayed on with me, so I give him free rein to plant what he pleases. Sometimes I think he forgets this place belongs to me."

"It is a showplace," said Lila nodding. "It must be

comforting to stroll through these lanes and to entertain in this garden."

"The only entertaining I've done has been for my employees. Perhaps I should plan a lawn party. Would you help me?"

"Oh, I don't know that I could. I mean, I . . ."

"You needn't look so terrified. You don't have to give the party tomorrow." He laughed and took her hand. "One minute I find you a very independent young woman, and the next you're a very vulnerable girl. You intrigue me, Miss Appleby." He led them down the path and into a stable area where a small colt lay nestled in the straw, trembling at the sound of them.

"For heaven's sake, here in the city. I'd never have dreamed of a colt being born here." Lila moved closer to see the tiny brown creature that stared back at her through enormous black eyes.

"Don't go too close. His mother might kick you, since she's very protective."

Lila was aware of his nearness as he stood behind her while she leaned on the stall door. If only she were as rich as the duchess, then perhaps she'd have a chance with him. No sooner had she thought that than he broke the spell with his next words.

"Ordinarily all the horses are sent to the country when they're with foal, but somehow Abigail slipped by. My head stableman has been out sick and the younger men weren't skilled enough to detect that Abigail was about to foal."

"Will she be all right here?"

"She will, but I'm afraid I will have to withdraw my invitation to take you to the races Saturday."

The disappointment overwhelmed Lila, but she tried to not show it. "Certainly. Don't think another thing about it." Her voice sounded colder than she intended.

"I was afraid you'd react this way. That's why I brought you here and showed you the colt. I knew your suspicious little mind would be thinking all manner of ill things about me, and you would probably never believe that I had to make a trip to my farm this weekend. Ordinarily I'd send the head stableman, but as I said, he's been down with the consumption for sometime now and isn't strong enough to make the trip. There's no possibility of sending one of the young lads alone. I take great pride in my horseflesh and wouldn't think of trusting such a move to one of them without my being along." He smiled at her, showing the deep cleft in his chin. "Am I forgiven?"

"Of course. Please don't worry about me." Lila turned to start for home.

"Wait and I'll walk back with you."

They didn't talk much on the trip back. Lila wanted to be cheerful and gay, but she simply couldn't think of anything to say. She hated the annoying habit of hers to become speechless at the most inopportune of times, but she found herself helpless to do anything about it.

When they reached her gate, she turned and bid him goodbye, abruptly ending all thought of further conversation. "I must go now. Aunt Maude made a list for me to carry to the store, and I need to make the trip before dark."

"Until my return," he said, tipping his hand in a farewell salute.

Lila walked to the house in an ill temper. He could have offered to drive her to Knightsbridge, knowing she didn't have a carriage. More important than that, he could have asked her to go to a race or to the gardens on another day.

To make Lila's melancholy greater, on Saturday morning she happened to be in the parlor when the duchess's carriage pulled up outside and Lord Whitfield came out and got into it. His own wagon containing the colt and mare followed behind as they set off for the country.

Lila groaned and felt a tear prick the corner of her eye. "Aunt Maude, I've been duped for certain. Lord Whitfield and the Duchess of Halstead must be spending the weekend at his country estate. I've been a saphead."

"Well, love, don't think too much about it. Maybe 'tis not what you think." Aunt Maude felt sorry for her niece. She too had secretly held out hopes that his lordship was interested in Lila.

"Men are an abomination! I shall stop thinking of suitors. Why did I allow myself to fall into such folly? The pain is more than I can bear." Lila stamped her foot, then dropped to the sofa and picked up the newspaper. "From this moment on I shall spend my time working for noble causes . . ."

"Humph! Like what?" asked Maude, shaking her head, while she tried to thread her needle.

"Like . . . like . . ." Lila skimmed the front page of the *London Times* trying to find some cause. Suddenly her

face brightened. "Like helping the poor. It says here
that there will be a town meeting of the tenants from
the slums to discuss the unfair rents and the poor con-
dition of their apartments." She folded the paper, so
that the article lay on top. "That settles it. I shall attend
the meeting tonight."

"My dear, you can't be serious. You aren't thinking
of going into the slums on Saturday?"

Lila shook her head. "No, of course not. Although
later I may tour the area to see for myself. There's a
town meeting to be held at St. Matthew's Church on
Brompton Road. I can take a hack there and back." She
stood and moved over to show Maude the article.

"If I can't talk you out of this nonsense, then I suppose I'll have to accompany you. I tell you, Lila, this is
not a wise decision. You need to think about this project for a few days. In fact, it's indelicate of me to mention this matter to you, but you really don't have the
funds to be too charitable to others."

"I don't have to contribute money. I am going to hear
what the speaker has to say. The *Times* says a great re-
former will be present at the meeting tonight."

"Mercy, but I don't like the sound of this." Maude
had a premonition no good could come from the avenue Lila seemed determined to pursue.

Chapter 13

LILA AND MAUDE arrived at St. Matthew's shortly before the seven o'clock meeting time and promptly took their seats in the meeting hall.

"I don't like the looks of this crowd one bit," whispered Maude as she scanned the small gathering. "They all look like pickpockets or worse."

"It's a good thing we don't have any jewelry with us." Lila studied the crowd, growing a bit uneasy about their safety. "What do you suppose those women do for a living?" She glanced at three women with bright orange-red hair, dressed in satin gowns which were soiled and patched. Around their shoulders they wore crocheted wraps in need of mending in several places.

"Exactly what you think they do." Maude reached for Lila's hand. "Come along, dear, we're going home. I will not be a part of this motley baggage."

For a moment Lila wavered, and then her resolve solidified. "No, we must stay. That's why we're here, to help these people fight their slum owners." Seeing the look of unease on her aunt's face, Lila weakened. "You go along if you like, but I'm going to stay. Besides, I think the vicar just arrived. You know nothing can harm us with him present."

"All I can say is I'm glad I left my money home. All they'll get is this pitiful old reticule."

Lila giggled and motioned for her to be quiet. The vicar called the group to attention and turned the meeting over to the night's speaker, who spoke eloquently on the rich keeping the poor in poverty. The more he talked about the wealthy, the less comfortable Lila began to feel. Somehow she didn't feel she belonged to this group any more than she did to the duchess's social strata. She was about ready to leave when the speaker began reading a list of slum owners. There at the top of the list were the Duchess of Halstead and Lord Whitfield, Earl of Wickambrook.

"Listen, Aunt Maude, they plan to picket Brighton Hall. That's next door." She giggled again nervously. "I'm going to sign up to join in the demonstration. I hope they don't discover that I'm Lord Whitfield's next door neighbor."

"Child, have you become an addlepate? You'll do no such thing. As your guardian, I order you to sit back down."

Whatever thin doubt there was in Lila's mind disappeared. Someone ordering her not to do something always had the opposite effect. She stood, and while Aunt Maude fanned herself vigorously, Lila marched to the front along with a few dozen other seedcakes and scrawled her name below several pitiful "X's." For a moment she hesitated to sign her real name and debated whether she should also scribble a simple "X," but pride won out and she wrote her full name with a flourish.

Once having accomplished this, she stood attentively, listening to the speaker's instructions. They were going to picket Lord Whitfield's home first, and that would be on the first Tuesday in the month.

Lila accepted the fact she was doing this because she was irritated with Lord Whitfield for going off to his country estate with the duchess. It was little grounds for such a retaliation, but the cause itself was a right one, so she held on to this principle. It was a great relief to her to hear the man say that the picketing would run from sun up until nightfall, but the picketers could choose their times, and no one was expected to stay the day if they had other things to do.

When the meeting was over Lila and Maude rode home in silence. Finally Maude could not hold her tongue another minute. "Young lady, I think you will be making a mistake to picket Lord Whitfield's house. He is our neighbor and until now has been a good friend. Don't you realize this will jeopardize our neighborly relationship?"

A mischievous grin crossed Lila's face. "Do you think he'll really be upset?"

"You need not take such relish in embarrassing the man." Maude shook her head and sighed deeply. "Honestly, I don't know what's come over you, Lila. You'd think His Lordship had done something to make you very angry."

Ignoring this, Lila argued, "Don't you think something needs to be done about the abominable conditions of these buildings? You heard how the man described them."

"If you want my honest opinion, and I can tell from the look in your eye that you don't, but I will give it to you anyhow. I didn't like the speaker tonight, nor the roguish bunch neither. No good can come from this. I'm a wise old woman, and I know when something's wrong."

Lila tried to console her aunt because she loved her very much and hated to see her agitated. She patted Maude's hand. "Now, now, I need a project to occupy my lonesome hours. Surely you can't begrudge me that."

"There's volunteering to write letters for the sick, or visiting shut-ins of our own class, but Lila, the group you'll be falling into looks a bit on the thieving side."

"Now, Aunt Maude, would the vicar of St. Matthew's have anything to do with a project that wasn't legal or morally proper?"

"I suppose you're right. But heed my warning: no good can come from this picketing business. Why, a person won't be safe to walk on the street in front of her own house. I can feel it in my bones. No good will come from this."

Lila didn't dare let her aunt know that she, too, was having a few qualms about the matter. And then she thought of Lord Whitfield and the duchess living lives of ease in their beautiful mansions while their tenants lived in squalor with rats and vermin, and she knew she was doing the right thing. Besides, wouldn't Lord

Whitfield be shocked when he saw her marching in the picket line in front of his house?

LILA WAS ABOUT to think Lord Whitfield would not get back from his country estate before the day set for the picket. She had been agitated over the matter for several days before she finally approached the subject with her aunt. They were sitting in the parlor, or Maude was sitting, quietly mending one of Lila's day dresses where she had ripped it on a nail, while Lila paced the floor.

"Do find a chair and sit down, Lila. You remind me of a caged cat, prancing from one end of the room to the other. What ails you anyway?"

"It doesn't look like Lord Whitfield is going to make it home before we're to picket outside his house."

"Be a blessing for us if he misses the fiasco. I still don't see the need for you to be involved in such." Maude's needle raced in and out of the fabric faster as she spoke. "This business of you in the street holding up a sign against your very own neighbor does not sit well with me."

"Where is your compassion? Don't you feel sorry for the poor tenants who are paying rent for those terrible buildings?"

"I say 'tis between Lord Whitfield and them. There are other things you could be doing to fill your—"

"Oh, Aunt Maude, he's back," whispered Lila, giggling nervously. She drew back the curtain to get a better view. "He appears in good spirits and rested." She looked to see if anyone else stepped down from the carriage. "I wonder where the duchess is?"

"Probably home minding her business like you should be. Now come away from that window. If you can't be decent to the man, then don't go snooping and spying on him."

"My, you are getting testy over this, aren't you?" But Lila did as her aunt said and dropped the curtain back in place, then moved over to pick up a book.

"I can tell when you're itching for an argument, and I'm not giving you one today. If your father was here, he'd put a stop to this nonsense."

"Well, he isn't, so stop fretting about that."

"Never thought a niece of mine would turn out to be a bluestocking. Doesn't sit too well in my craw, that's all."

THE NEXT TWO days were uneventful, and as soon as classes ended on Tuesday afternoon, Lila raced up to her room and got her bonnet and a light shawl. A slow drizzle had fallen since early morn and she was not overly thrilled at having to stand in it until sundown, but she had signed up for this time and she knew she had to go.

"I see you're determined to go, even if you catch your death." Maude stood in the hall as Lila came downstairs.

"Aunt Maude, please don't be so upset. Nothing is going to happen to me. I promise."

"It wouldn't surprise me if you got kidnapped by that crew and dragged into the slums to be some man's doxie." Maude had the Appleby blood in her veins, and she intended to fight to prevent this mistake any way she could.

"Why, Aunt Maude, I never dreamed you even knew about such things. I'm impressed." Lila took her shawl off the peg and threw it around her shoulders. She headed toward the back of the house.

"Where are you going?"

"I've got to sneak out the back door and come from around the corner. I don't want those people to think I live next door to a slum owner." With that, Lila's gown vanished around the corner and the back door slammed.

Maude moved to the window to see what was transpiring outside. She waited patiently until she saw Lila join the group, shake hands with a tall stranger, and accept a sign from him. If she stood at the window, she at least would know Lila was safe. Everything appeared to be quiet. Lord Whitfield wasn't home, and no servant had come out to run off the crowd.

What Maude did not know, however, was that all bedlam had broken out at Brighton Hall. The head butler, Albert, upon seeing the picket forming that morning, had sent a servant to Parliament to bring home Lord Whitfield.

Whitfield was scheduled to address his peers on an important issue that morning, so upon receiving the message simply sent the lad on to the sheriff to request the crowd be dispersed from in front of his house, or if the sheriff deemed it necessary, that they be arrested and carted off to jail. The sheriff, who had been out of the city chasing a horse thief, did not return to his office until minutes before Lila took up her post.

Therefore, within thirty minutes of Lila beginning her march, the sheriff, along with the jail cart, arrived on the scene. Aunt Maude stood in front of the window and watched in horror as Lila was herded into the wagon along with the other picketers. The last thing she saw of Lila was her glancing toward the Appleby house with a stricken look on her face.

Maude raced to the front door and down the steps, but the wagon pulled away as she screamed for it to halt. Of course the pounding of the horses' hooves drowned out the gentlewoman's frantic cries.

"Merciful heavens, what must I do?" Maude stood and wrung her hands.

She rushed back into her house, put on her bonnet, and set out for Lord Whitfield's. There was nothing to do but wait for his arrival home and plead with him to go save Lila. She was not at all certain he would do such a noble thing. Perhaps if she pleaded that Lila was touched in the head. She drew a deep breath and set off for Brighton Hall.

Chapter 14

LORD WHITFIELD FINISHED his eloquent plea for fairer Poor Laws and felt satisfied with his day's work. He then decided he needed to be on his way home to see if the emergency had been properly handled. Albert sometimes tended to overreact in a crisis.

When Whitfield's carriage pulled up in front of his house he felt relief, because the street was empty and there was no sign of trouble. Even the late afternoon sun had appeared from behind a cloud, so he stepped from the carriage without any idea of the bedlam to follow.

Albert opened the front door before Lord Whitfield had touched the brass knocker. "Good afternoon, my lord. I'm so relieved to see you home, sir. There's a lady in the study waiting to see you, and if I may say so, sir, she's highly agitated."

"Who is she, Albert?"

"Mrs. Maude Watson from next door." He took Whitfield's cloak and top hat.

"Something must have happened to Lila." The color drained from Whitfield's cheeks, and he rushed off down the hall forcing Albert to run to get there in time to open the door for him.

"Mrs. Watson, what is it? Has something happened to Lila?"

Maude dabbed at a tear, her face splotchy from crying. Lord Whitfield took her hands in his and put his arm around her, comforting her as best he could. "Please, please, you must stop crying long enough to tell me what has happened. I can't understand a word you're saying, you're babbling on so."

"Lila's been arrested and taken off to jail." There she'd said it, and she blew her nose loudly as if to emphasize the atrocity of the situation.

"Lila? In jail? I don't understand." He looked from Maude to Albert, who still stood nearby.

"I think, my lord, that Miss Appleby was in the group of picketers you had the sheriff cart away."

"What was she doing in that motley bunch? I still don't understand."

"That sir, I think only Mrs. Watson can explain." The butler and Whitfield stared at Maude, waiting for an explanation.

"Lila got some silly notion that she wanted to help the poor and she made me attend a meeting with her. At the meeting they decided to picket owners of slum dwellings." Maude didn't know how much to tell Lord Whitfield for fear he'd grow angrier and not help her at all. There wasn't another gentleman she knew who might be able to get Lila out of that terrible jail. The tears began flowing again. "I tried to stop her I'm so sorry . . ."

Hugh's jaw tensed as he struggled to not lose his temper. He knew this was not the time to explode and point out what a ninny Maude had been not to come and tell him Lila was contemplating such a stupid and dangerous action.

"Listen, you go back home and wait for me." Turning to Albert he ordered, "Bring my carriage around front quickly. I must go get Miss Appleby before . . . before . . ." He didn't finish the sentence. Instead he glanced from Albert to Maude and back, but the butler understood.

"Now Mrs. Watson, when Albert returns I'll have him see you home. You wait there until I return with Lila."

"Can you get her out of . . . j-jail?" She could scarce bear to say the terrible word.

"I give you my word on that. And when I get through giving Miss Appleby a tongue lashing, she'll think twice before doing such an addlepated thing again."

Maude put her hand on Hugh's arm and tried to think of something to say on Lila's behalf. "Sir, she didn't mean to harm you. I know that. It's simply that she hasn't enough to do and grows bored with so much idle time on her hands." She shrugged and wiped at a tear. "What she needs is a home, a husband, and babies to keep her busy."

"You are exactly correct, Mrs. Watson, and I shall do something about this so that it never happens again.

We can't have Lila racing about the city carrying placards and fighting causes . . ."

Albert returned to the door with Lord Whitfield's cape and hat. "Your carriage is ready, sir. And good luck in rescuing Miss Appleby."

"Thank you, Albert. Please see that Mrs. Watson gets home safely, and instruct her cook to prepare a pot of tea and to start water boiling for Miss Appleby. I have an idea that when she gets out of that jail she's going to want a hot bath." He heard Maude sniffle, so he hushed.

Night had descended upon the city and a thick fog began to roll in, making it difficult for Whitfield to even see the lamplighters as they moved through the city lighting the street lights. "To the jail," ordered Hugh, "and drive as fast as you can."

He took his seat as the carriage jerked into motion. The sound of the horses' hooves on the cobbled street and the squeaking of carts as peddlers closed up shop and moved home for the night were the only sounds to distract Whitfield from the thoughts that raged through him. What if something had happened to his Lila? She was the most adorable, frustrating, irritating creature he'd ever known, but she fascinated him, and even though he had stayed on his country estate and thrown himself into the tasks of running his lands, still she had crept into his thoughts.

The thought of what she might be going through at the hands of the jailers who would readily spot that she was not a common street baggage, made him pound on the roof of the carriage with his cane, urging his driver to even faster speeds. The black carriage with the gold crest of the Earl of Wickambrook sped through the city at breakneck speed. Whitfield rocked from side to side as the carriage swayed around corners, striking a pothole from time to time. At last the lights of the jail loomed in the distance and he began to relax for the first time.

The carriage wheels had scarce stopped turning when Whitfield bounded from inside and charged up the steps of the large brick building past several men loitering around outside chatting and smoking.

LILA HOVERED IN the corner of a large holding room along with a group of about twenty other women, most grimy, smelly creatures who scratched at some part of their bodies constantly. She thought she might have a case of the hysterics, when suddenly she heard a loud booming voice she recognized immediately. Her spirits soared and she jumped up and ran to the bars, straining to hear what was happening outside.

"I say open this door at once! I'm the Earl of Wickambrook and I've come for Miss Lila Appleby. Are you deaf, man? Move out of my way. The jailer has my papers. I want this woman, this lady, freed at once."

A key scraped in the lock and suddenly the door sprang open. Lila ran into Whitfield's arms. "I'm so thankful to see you."

"Come, let's be away from this vile smelling place." Whitfield wrapped Lila in his strong arms and hugged her tightly.

"Take me, sir. I kin show you a far better evenin' than this scrawny hag," called a dirty-faced doxie. She cackled at her own joke and several other women also called to the earl.

Once they were in the carriage, Lila finally gave way to the hysteria she'd felt for hours. Crying quietly, she sniffled because she'd not only lost her handkerchief, but her reticule as well, and had not dared to stop to repossess any of her belongings for fear of being detained in that horrible place another minute.

Whitfield, who was so angry with her now that she was safe, wanted to take her in his arms and shake her until she begged for mercy, but finally relented and pulled out his handkerchief and handed it to her.

"I-I'm so thankful to b-be out of that place," she sobbed, blowing her nose loudly. "Thank you for coming and getting me. I didn't know what was going to happen to me."

Finally, Whitfield could stand the tears no longer, so he put his arm around her and pulled her near. "Hush, hush, you're safe now," he crooned to her, caressing her hair back from her wet cheeks.

She continued to sniffle, but she lay her head on his shoulder. It felt so good to be in the comforting arms of the man she loved so much. But of course, she dared not tell him that. Instead she said, "I'm sorry I picketed your house. I just want . . . wanted . . . to help the poor."

"Phew! But you do smell, my dear. Did they dip you in the gutter or something?" He wrinkled his nose against the acrid odor which permeated her clothing.

"My gown is ruined," she moaned, fingering a tear and black spot of dirt, then she giggled. "I do smell awful, don't I? They shoved us all in the jail cart and I fell on the floor. I'm afraid it wasn't very clean."

"Well, nothing a good bath and a clean gown can't remedy. Just be thankful the jailers didn't take a liking to you."

"What about the others? They meant you no harm."

"No harm? They want to destroy my property and stop paying rent which is a part of my income. You call that nothing?" His temper began to flare again. "I should have had the lot of you thrown into Newgate Prison. How would you like that?"

She sat up straight and her anger began to rise also. "It wasn't fair to rescue me and not the others. We must go back. Tell the driver to turn around."

He shook his head and glared at her. "You are the most obstinate woman I've ever known. We are not turning around." Seeing that she was struggling with the carriage door latch, he drew her back into the seat and said, "If you must know, I instructed the jailer to free the lot. I only asked that he give me time to leave the premises first in case there was a disturbance. All I need on my conscience is the killing of some slum beggar."

Lila grinned saucily. "You aren't the ogre you pretend to be, are you?"

"I am when people meddle into my business, so be forewarned. Now, here we are. Let's go in and show your aunt that you're uninjured and no harm came to anything other than your pride."

The front door flew open and Maude greeted them as they came up the steps, rushing to enfold Lila in her arms. "Thank heavens you're safe. I nearly went mad worrying about you. Young lady, I'm putting my foot down. This will end your bluestocking antics. What will the *ton* think if they hear you've been arrested?" She herded the two into the parlor. "Oh, Lila, love, don't sit down." Maude held a handkerchief to her nose. "Run along upstairs. I'll ring for Rose to bring you a hot bath. Lord Whitfield warned us to have the water hot."

Lila turned to leave, but not before she paused beside Lord Whitfield and extended her hand. "Please, sir, accept my apologies for my cakey behavior and thank you for rescuing me. I must confess that staying one more minute in that jail would probably have brought about a complete nervous collapse on my part. It was most abominable." She curtsied and then looked up into his smiling face. "And I can understand if you wish to have no more to do with me as a neighbor, so I wish you and the duchess the best of happiness." She turned and ran lightly upstairs.

The smile on Lord Whitfield's face vanished at her last words and he turned to Maude. "What does she mean by that?"

"I wouldn't hold much store in anything she says tonight, other than that she is deeply grateful, as I am, for your rescuing her. Really, Lord Whitfield, I don't know what I would have done had you not come home to help me."

"I hope she has learned a sound lesson. You realize, Mrs. Watson, that what she needs is a husband and a house to run for him."

Maude brightened. "Indeed she does, sir. Her father gave her far too many liberties when he was alive, and now she is not easy to control." Cutting her eyes over at him slyly, she continued. "You don't have someone in mind for her, do you, by any chance?"

"Perhaps," he replied, standing to leave. He took Maude's hand and kissed it. "Now I must be on my way so you can go up and see about our wayward charge."

"I hope things will settle down around here now and get back to normal. There's been far too much excitement for an old lady in the past two weeks."

Chapter 15

THE FOLLOWING DAY Lila was up and dressed early, completely recovered from her experience of the previous day. She put on a bright green gown and tied her clean, thick hair back with a green ribbon. She even sprinkled a few drops of rose water on her neck and wrists, trying to be certain all traces of the jail smells had vanished forever. While she had appeared calm when she left Lord Whitfield, she had tossed and turned with nightmares throughout the night.

In the bright sunlight of the morning she was suddenly filled with anxiety over whether rumors of her arrest might sift out into the *ton*, for there was nothing they enjoyed more than a bit of scandalous gossip. Suddenly she chilled at the thought that there might even be an article in the *Times* about the incident. Ringing for Rose, she gave her a coin and sent her out to fetch the latest editions of the London newspapers.

But Lila could have saved her fretting over her own

reputation, because things were already spinning out of her control.

The girls arrived promptly at ten and the lessons commenced without any hint that things were other than usual. After the noon meal Jacinda asked if the girls might go for a stroll in the garden, and Lila, whose nerves were still raw, gladly consented, instructing them to return at one-thirty. She, in turn, went upstairs to lie down and rest for the short time they would be gone. Even Maude decided to take a short nap. All of this was as it had been many times before.

But when Lila came down for the afternoon classes, she found the parlor empty. Going out into the garden she called to the girls, and Idelia and Hortense answered immediately.

"Come along, girls." She glanced around, her heart sinking. "Where is Jacinda?"

Both girls giggled and glanced at one another.

Lila put her hands on her hips and glared at them. "Has she gone off to Lord Whitfield's again to meet Lord Haydon? This is not a day for her to try my patience." She started off toward the garden gate.

"Miss Appleby, she isn't over there." Hortense handed Lila a note. "She asked me to give you this."

Thoroughly puzzled, Lila stared at the note for a moment, turning it over and recognizing Jacinda's expert penmanship. "Is this some kind of game you girls have thought up?"

"No ma'am. Jacinda has eloped with Lord Haydon." Idelia became frightened when she saw the color drain from Lila's face. "I wanted to tell you, but Hortense said that she'd box my ears soundly if I ruined Jacinda's chance at happiness." She stuck out her tongue at her older sister.

"Are you all right, Miss Appleby?" asked Hortense, seeing how pale she had turned.

"I just need to sit for a moment until I recover from the shock." Lila put her hand to her forehead while she nervously spread open the note with her other hand.

The note read:

Dear Miss Appleby,
    By the time you read this I will be out of the city with my lover. Lord Haydon and I will be married in a proper ceremony when we reach Scotland, but until then our whereabouts will be secret. I am sorry I had to do this, but there was no other way. We love each other very much, yet Papa refuses to consent to our match. I know that I've let you down, but my future happiness depends on spending the rest of my life with Robert.
                                    Your humble student,
                                    Jacinda
P.S. Oh, and you are the best teacher I ever had. I shall name my first daughter Lila and always will remember you in my heart with fondness.

"She also left a note for you to give to her parents." Hortense handed it over to Lila, who put it in her pocket.

"Girls, I'll leave you here with Aunt Maude. I must get a hack and go tell Jacinda's parents."

When they came rushing into the parlor, all talking

at once, Maude heard all the commotion and her name being called, so she came hurrying down the stairs to meet them. "What is wrong? Has one of the girls been hurt?"

"Jacinda has eloped!" cried the Penkridge girls in unison.

Maude's hand flew to her mouth and she looked over at Lila, who nodded that it was true. "What are you going to do, Lila?"

"I'm going next door and see if Lord Whitfield is home. Perhaps he will accompany me to tell Mr. and Mrs. Kingsbury." She gritted her teeth. "It's the least he can do after having that scapegallows for a friend and allowing him to loiter around Brighton Hall all the time just waiting for Jacinda to appear."

"Now don't be too hard on Lord Haydon. Jacinda didn't seem to be running from him."

"Maybe her parents will be happy to have her married and off their hands. She was a sly puss."

"Let's assume they are very much in love and her parents will give them their blessings."

"Somehow I doubt that. Mr. Kingsbury knew Haydon needed money, and Jacinda will inherit a fortune." Lila threw on her bonnet and tied its ribbons quickly. "No, I fear I'm in for a dressing down that will curl your toes."

Maude held open the door for Lila. "Remind them that they will be gaining an earl for a son-in-law."

"I doubt I'll have time to put up much of an argument for the man. Mr. Kingsbury will probably ride hell-for-leather to find them and stop the wedding."

"Do you think he's likely to succeed?"

"Not if they don't want to be found." Lila squeezed Maude's hand before turning to run down the steps.

She rushed over to Brighton Hall and pounded on the door.

Albert opened the door after an interminably long wait. "Good day, Miss Appleby."

"Albert, I need to see Lord Whitfield immediately. May I come in?" Lila rushed into the hallway before Albert could step aside. She started down the corridor not waiting to be announced.

"I'm sorry, ma'am, but His Lordship is not at home."

Lila spun around and cried, "Not home! Oh, no. Do you know where he went?"

"That I don't, ma'am. He said that he was going in to see his solicitor on business. I know that Mr. Weathersby practices on Cromwell Road. You might see his carriage there."

"Oh, thank you, Albert. Do you suppose you could hail me a carriage? It's very urgent that I get downtown."

"Of course, Miss Appleby." He bowed and started out the door with Lila behind him. She thought he was exceptionally slow today, but knew it was probably her impatience.

Within minutes she was seated in the carriage, which started off at a brisk pace. She tried to catch her breath and decide what she would say to the Kingsburys. As the coach sped toward the inner city, Lila watched out the window for Lord Whitfield or his carriage, but he was nowhere to be seen.

They finally reached Cromwell Road, and had turned east on it, when Lila spotted a familiar figure ahead. It was Lord Whitfield. She was about to tap on the roof of the carriage to get the driver to stop when she saw he was not alone. The Duchess of Halstead stood behind Whitfield, dressed in a bright red gown with matching pelisse, and the couple was engrossed in conversation. Lila shrank back in the carriage seat as they rushed past, but not before she caught a glimpse of Whitfield putting his arm around the duchess and handing her into his carriage. The sight made Lila flinch unconsciously and her spirits fell even lower.

Lord Whitfield had been so besotted by the duchess that he had not even glanced around as the hack sped by. Lila realized how foolish she had been to harbor any hopes that he might choose her over someone as beautiful and worldly as the duchess. A tiny tear trickled down her cheek and she wiped at it with a daintily gloved hand. There was nothing to do but continue on and face Mr. Kingsbury alone.

Since it was early afternoon, she decided to go to his place of business and ask to speak with him. It might be wiser for him to go home and break the news to his wife.

The coach stopped in front of Mr. Kingsbury's brokerage house and she descended the steps nervously. Although she knew he owned the King's Bank, she had heard Jacinda say that he spent most of his time here at the brokerage.

"Please wait for me," she said to the driver. This trip would cost her a pretty penny, but it couldn't be helped she thought in her usual logical manner.

When Lila entered the office, which smelled of tobacco smoke and pine wood, a clerk glanced up from his ledger and leaped to his feet. Ladies were not a common sight in this man's world of cotton trading.

"May I help you, ma'am?"

"Yes. I'm here to see Mr. Kingsbury. Please tell him that Miss Lila Appleby is here and it's very urgent that I speak with him at once." Lila paced the floor while she awaited the clerk's return.

Within a few minutes, Mr. Kingsbury came rushing out of his office behind the clerk. He took Lila's hand in his and said, "Miss Appleby, what can I do for you? Nothing has happened to Jacinda, has there?"

Glancing around, Lila saw that the clerk was back at his desk, but listening with curiosity. "I must speak to you alone, Mr. Kingsbury."

"Of course." He led the way into his private office and offered Lila a chair across from his large mahogany desk. "Now, please tell me what your problem is. Can I do something for you?"

"Mr. Kingsbury, Jacinda has run off with Lord Haydon. She left this letter for you and Mrs. Kingsbury."

" 'Pon my word! You can't be serious, woman. Jacinda and that fortune hunter?"

"He is an earl, sir. It could be worse. They did appear to be in love." What else had Maude told her to say?

"You're an addlepate talking about love. Love has nothing to do with making a good match. Jacinda is beautiful. She could have married a duke had she been trained properly in the skills of the *ton* as I hired you to do. You'll be ruined when I get through with you, young woman. That much I promise you." He glared at her as though he might strike her, and Lila moved out of his reach.

"His home, Wexford House, is reputed to be lovely." She was babbling and she knew it, yet she couldn't stop. "I really am sorry, sir. I . . . I tried to watch her as closely as possible."

"You did a sorry job of it, if you ask me. Come along, woman. I've got to go tell Mrs. Kingsbury and go for the constable. Maybe we can catch them before they get too far." He rang for the clerk to fetch his cloak and his carriage. "How long have they been gone?" he thundered.

Lila had a strange urge to remind him she was not deaf, but thought better of it. Instead she swallowed hard and glanced at the wall clock that hung in the outer office. "A good two or two and a half hours, sir."

"Blast it, woman! What took you so long?"

Fortunately he dashed out the door before she could answer, leaving her standing wide eyed and speechless. Finally she shook her head in disbelief that all this was happening to her and turned to find her carriage. With relief she instructed the driver to take her back home and climbed inside. Falling back on the carriage seat, she thought things couldn't get much worse.

It was eleven o'clock the next morning before she learned how wrong she was.

It took Lila several minutes to calm Hortense and Idelia and to start classes. There was no word of Jacinda and Lord Haydon, so the group assumed they had outrun the constable and Mr. Kingsbury.

Maude and Lila were suffering through a duet by

the Penkridge sisters when there came a loud banging on the front door. Lila looked from Maude to the girls in utter bewilderment.

"It's Papa," cried Idelia who'd gone to the window to peep out. "What's he doing here? He looks furious, Hortense."

"I'm sure it's nothing," said Lila, standing and moving quickly to the front door.

"Where are my two girls?" Penkridge roared, shoving past Nettie and storming into the parlor. Seeing the girls, he ordered, "Get your things together, we're going home."

"But Papa, we like Miss Appleby's school." Hortense moved close to her father. "You aren't taking us out of our classes, are you?"

"I most certainly am. Now do as I command and go wait for me in the carriage. I want a few words with this woman."

The girls scurried to gather their wraps and books, waving to Miss Appleby and Maude as they dashed out the door.

"What appears to be the problem?" Lila asked the question, but she already could guess the answer.

"The very idea of you pretending to be a school teacher when you live such a sordid life yourself. If you've besmirched my pure daughters with your carrying on, I'll have you horsewhipped and run out of London. I can promise you one thing—you'll never teach another innocent young lady."

"Mr. Penkridge, I think it's extremely unfair to place the sole blame on me for Miss Kingsbury's elopement.

I can scarcely be responsible for watching her every second."

"That's scandalous enough. She tricked her father. Instead of going to Scotland, they slipped off to Bath and married slick as you please. A message arrived this morning stating that it was too late to stop them now." He shook his head. "But that's not the worst. Mr. Kingsbury paid me a visit this morning to inform me that you had spent time in jail as recently as last week. Imagine, a common criminal caring for my innocents."

The color drained from Lila's cheeks. "Sir, it really isn't as bad as it sounds. I . . . that is . . . we . . ." She glanced toward Maude to come to her rescue, but the elderly woman stood as still as if she'd been cast in stone.

"Do you deny you were in the local jail?" He stalked to Lila's side and glared down at her. "Are you calling Mr. Kingsbury and the constable a liar?"

"No, no, they are partially correct." Seeing the glint of satisfaction cross his face, Lila simply stopped. What was the point of losing her pride too?

"Good day, Miss Appleby. And I suggest you take down that silly sign outside. Your school is officially closed, or I shall return with the constable and have you arrested for . . . for . . . I'll think of some charge which will put you away for years." With that, he stalked out of the house and was gone.

Lila sat down with a jolt and stared at Maude. "What are we to do? My school is destroyed. I have only a few pounds left to my name, and my reputation will be ruined when the Penkridges get through telling all the *ton* about my being in jail." She shook her head in bewilderment. "I can't believe this is happening to me."

Maude came over to her side and patted Lila's hand. "There, there, I never did care much for those silly girls anyhow. A life of teaching the likes of those three would have put you in an early grave."

Lila giggled. "The Penkridge girls were awful, weren't they? Couldn't carry a tune or conjugate a French verb to save themselves." Then a tear trickled down her cheek. "But I loved them, Aunt Maude. Even that wild Jacinda. I knew she was trouble the moment I set eyes on her, but she was sweet, too." She wiped at a tear and blew her nose noisily.

"Listen, we'll pack up here and go back to Leeds. You can start again there with some other profession. Who knows," Maude said more cheerfully than she felt, "you might even find some nice widower and wed."

"That would be a lark," said Lila, sniffing loudly.

Chapter 16

THE FOLLOWING MORNING, after spending a restless night, Lila rose and dressed quickly. She decided to take out her prettiest rose gown and wear it. What did it matter? She was on her way to the poor house anyway—why not wear something that would cheer her?

The bright morning sun had a way of boosting her spirits, and during the night as she'd tossed, she had come to several important decisions. First she would list her house with a broker, next she would pack and go home with Aunt Maude for a while, third and most important of all, she'd try very hard to find a good, kind widower, preferably without daughters—she giggled—and she'd marry him. Never again would she fill her mind with fantasies of love and . . . and Lord Whitfield. She knew he was unobtainable.

She also decided that she was happy for Jacinda. She

had married the man she loved, which had to be better than marrying someone your parents chose for you.

Having come to these worldly decisions, Lila's spirits rose and she marched off to town to list her property with a broker. Once that was accomplished, she came home and placed the huge FOR SALE sign in her front yard.

When she came back in the house she called to Maude: "I've done it, so let's start packing now. I want to leave the city as soon as possible."

Lila and Maude spent the next two days sorting through Lila's meager possessions, trying to decide what should be moved and what could remain to be sold with the house.

It was late afternoon on the third day when someone knocked on Lila's front door. Not waiting for Nettie to come answer, Lila brushed a lock of hair from out of her eyes, blew a smudge of lint from her nose, and marched to the door to open it.

"Lord Whitfield!" she exclaimed in shock.

"What do you think you're doing?" he demanded, staring down at her.

"Please come in," she replied calmly. "I'm not dressed for company, but I don't suppose that matters anymore. My appearance matches my reputation." She was really too dejected to care how he thought she looked. And what did it matter anyhow? She was nothing compared to the duchess, who always appeared stylish and her hair coiffured to perfection.

"What is the meaning of that sign in your yard? And what of your school? I've been busy the last few days, but Albert tells me you closed your school and are going away."

"That's correct. Do you wish to sit or do you prefer to stand and glare at me? Whichever is fine with me. I've been berated so much this week that nothing you say will have the least effect on me." She moved airily over to a chair and sat down. "However, I've been working hard, and I need to rest for a minute, so I shall sit here and prop my feet on this stool while you rant and rave." She waved her hand. "Proceed when ready."

Maude moved out of the room and into the kitchen. She saw immediately that she was not needed in the parlor. Whatever was on Lord Whitfield's mind did not concern her.

"I asked you about the sign in the front yard." He glared down at her, his hands placed firmly on his hips.

"Surely you aren't dimwitted. That's a for sale sign. It means that my house is for sale and I'm going away."

"You can't do that."

"I don't see why not."

"Because I hold a mortgage on this property." He grinned rakishly, a twinkle in his eyes.

Lila's eyes flew open in shock. "You what?" She shook her head. "That's impossible."

"Oh, is it?" He withdrew his wallet and took out the promissory note he'd bought off Haydon. "Is this not your father's signature?"

Lila snatched the paper from his hands and read it quickly. "I can't believe this. I had no idea." She looked up at him suspiciously. "Why haven't you presented this before now?"

"Because I knew you were stubborn and head-strong, and I had a feeling it would serve me better later. It seems I was correct."

"Well, take my house. That will make me scarce poorer than I am now." Lila said this with a confidence she didn't feel. Without the money from the sale, she was as poor as a church mouse.

"I have no need to take possession of this house at present, however, you must stay here until I am ready to do so."

"And why, pray tell, should I do such a foolish thing?"

"Because I will have you arrested for evading a debt if you don't." He knew this was not likely to happen, but he was desperate to keep her in town until he could woo her and make her see that he loved her. "My solicitor will need time to untangle this property."

"And how long will this take?"

He shrugged. "Oh, perhaps a few weeks or months. Solicitors are very busy people and the courts move slowly."

She stood and faced him. "Well, if you say it's the law, then I suppose I'll have to stay. But I do beseech you to speed this along as quickly as possible."

He bowed and said, "Good day, Miss Appleby. I shall be coming over from time to time to inspect my property to make certain you aren't doing damage to it."

"If you'll let me know when you're coming, I'll be out of the house," said Lila, equally formally. The very sight of him made her heart beat faster. Couldn't he see she was madly in love with him and had to get as far away as possible?

Lord Whitfield departed and Lila called to her aunt: "We might as well quit packing for today. Lord Whitfield ordered me to remain in town until this debt is cleared." With that Lila marched off to her room to sulk and plot. Suppose she made herself such an undesirable neighbor that he'd be glad to see her leave?

The following morning Lila's spirits soared as she decided what she intended to do to upset Lord Whitfield. Putting on her oldest dress, she set out to the gardener's shed to find some old paint. Once she had located it, she took down the for sale sign and began repainting it. When she had finished, she stepped back and admired her handiwork.

By late afternoon the paint had dried and Lila got a hammer and drove the sign back into the ground, then went back inside pleased with her success. She listened for Lord Whitfield's carriage. When it arrived she peeped out the window to see him staring over at her house, a look of horror on his face. She giggled as he stormed across the distance to her front door.

On his second knock, she opened the door and said sweetly, "Come in, Lord Whitfield. Have you come to inspect your holdings?" She gestured around her innocently. "As you can see I haven't knocked holes in the walls, nor nailed the furniture to the floor."

"Miss Appleby, what is the meaning of that new sign in your yard? I don't have time for pranks, young lady."

"That's not a prank, sir. I am in earnest. I must have some way to support myself until I leave London."

"You will not open a kennel for dogs here, next door to my house. I absolutely forbid it!" His face turned red and he glared down at her with a look which would have caused most to wither. "I ought to—"

She stared up at him with innocent blue eyes, batting her lashes slyly.

"—to marry you. Confound you, woman, but you need a man to make you behave and I'm just the one to do it." He grinned down at her. "A spanking every now and then might do you good."

"That's a horrible thing to say." But her heart was pounding, and she thought her heart might burst with joy. "Besides, you've said nothing of love, and I'd never marry a man who didn't love me."

He took her in his arms and said, "You are an impossible creature, but I have loved you from afar for months."

"You have?" She gasped in shock. "But what about the Duchess of Halstead?" She stood cradled in his arms and made no effort to free herself.

"The duchess? We are merely friends. Whatever made you think I was in love with her?"

"I saw her at your house often." Her chin jutted out stubbornly. "And you went away with her to your country estate. I saw her carriage the day you left."

"Mine had a broken axle. She gave me a ride to my estate since she goes right past on the way to hers."

"And just last week I saw you talking to her on the street and you both got in your carriage."

"We were discussing that messy business about our

being slum owners and were on our way to our manager to see how he was coming with improving our tenements."

"You were?"

"Yes, does that please you?" He groaned. "You probably won't be satisfied until I've given away the last pound to my name."

"No, that won't be necessary." She grinned up at him slyly.

"So what is your answer? Will you marry me?"

Lila smiled at him and nodded. "Yes, oh, yes." She slid her arms around his neck and turned up her lips to receive his kiss. The warm touch of his lips on hers sent a thrill charging through her body, and she clung to him, savoring the sensation. When at last they broke apart, he said, "We shall be married as soon as the banns can be posted. However, I must warn you, I want a house full of children, and my heirs may be a handful."

"Humm," she said coyly, "I've tamed worse."

And when he looked about to argue, she leaned forward and kissed him boldly, a feat which quieted him immediately.